CLAIMED
BY THE
CREATURE

INTERNATIONAL BESTSELLING AUTHOR

SARAH SPADE

FOREWORD

Thank you for checking out *Claimed by the Creature*!

This is the fifth book in the **Sombra Demons** series and, like the others, can be read as a standalone. It's also part of a new arc that will conclude in book six, *Grabbed by the Guard*, as well as in the upcoming novella *Drawn to the Demon Duke* (which is technically going to be both a prequel and extended epilogue that ties the whole series together when it finally releases this summer!). So while a few characters from earlier books make a short cameo in this story, it truly belongs to Dagon and Sierra (and, okay, Three).

Claimed by the Creature tells the story of a super famous pop star and the shadow demon who is fated to be her one true mate. This book features the fated mates trope, a sweet yet undoubtedly possessive demon, a slightly meddlesome ex in one chapter, a stalker of a fan in another, explicit sex scenes, some profanity, and a ton of instalove over their weekend together. It's specifically written for adult readers who like a little fluff and some spice with their monster romance—and I hope you enjoy it!

xoxo,
Sarah

CHAPTER 1
SIERRA'S PRISON

SIERRA

In the long run, I guess it could've always been worse.

Most people, when they have a nervous break-down, end up in a psych hospital.

Me? When I did, my prison became the penthouse apartment of the Dorado, located on the Upper West Side of Manhattan. I have my best friend here with me—oh, and Billie, too, who wouldn't even question me claiming Three first—and my security team's solemn promise that no one will be able to bother me so long as I don't leave the building.

After what happened to me? I haven't even left the actual *apartment* yet.

I have no reason to. It's a classic six, one floor below

the rooftop. It has a living room with a TV so huge, it's like a movie theater; a master bedroom for me, one for Billie, and a spare guest room for when Roy needs to be on-site; a kitchen; a study/library that is Billie's sanctuary; and the gallery which is a fancy name for the hallway that is plastered with photos of all four of my album covers. As much as I love it and consider it home, I rarely get to stay here, and though I'm getting cabin fever lately, both halves of me were desperate for the peace.

The peace, plus the time to think... I definitely need it—and not just because my mental health is shot.

To the world, I'm Whiskey Rose.

When I'm home, I get to be Sierra Landry.

These days, I'm not sure *who* I want to be—and I can trace it back to what happened in California.

It's been nearly three weeks since I had a public meltdown during one of the first nights on this leg of my world tour. Three weeks since it was put on hold, my fans all being told that I would reschedule the dates at a later time. Three weeks since I flew back to Manhattan, holing up in here with Three, Billie, and sometimes Roy. My ENT—with an emphasis on the T —comes to me. So do my lawyers, therapists, and anyone else who needs to meet with me while I'm 'resting'.

Most of them deal with Billie. As my closest friend

and my long-time manager, Billie Bickles is almost as protective of me as Roy Saunders is. I swear, if she could pop open her mouth and let Dr. Martin check out her larynx instead of mine, she would. After all, having spent her formative years singing right alongside me, she knows the drill.

She knows how serious a vocal injury is—just like she knows how rough it can be to be the subject of countless blind items, tabloid pieces, and Internet articles, all because I freaked out one time in front of a crowd of *thousands*.

More than that, Billie knows my history. She doesn't blame me for losing it, not when I swore I spotted the one face in the crowd that never should've been there...

Patrick Ridgefield is supposed to be in lock-up, waiting for his trial. My top lawyer got in touch with the DA and arranged it so that it didn't start until after my world tour wrapped up in August. Despite my name and her pull, there's not going to be any getting out of testifying against my former stalker, but at least I could make it through my tour before dealing with that.

And then, three weeks ago, I was convinced I picked out his face in the crowd, the only fan not singing along as I was in the middle of one of my hits.

I saw him. In the same breath, I was thrown back to last summer when Patrick Ridgefield—wearing nothing but an open hooded sweatshirt, dark jeans, and a picture with my face plastered on the front—ambushed me outside of Bow Tie Cinemas during a press showing for *Jessica's Journey*, my debut film role. He pulled a gun out of his sweatshirt, aiming it at me, and if it wasn't for Roy's crew taking point on my security, he would've killed me.

He didn't. Obviously. Kyle, Gino, and Jeff tackled him while Roy hustled Billie and me away from the scene before the gun could go off. That didn't make hearing Ridgefield's confession any easier to swallow when the DA came to me for questioning.

Patrick Ridgefield had been stalking me for eight years at that point. Going to every one of my concerts, following my career obsessively from the time I was a member of Thr33peat to my breaking out and going solo—and I had no clue.

Still, I could deal with that... but Ridgefield was also the reason one of my beloved cats went missing while I was in Europe five years ago, and that I can *never* forgive.

It kills me to think about what happened. Having paid off the petsitter I hired for the couple of months Billie and I were gone, he stole Two, keeping her as his own until she somehow died—and then he had her stuffed and positioned as part of a shrine dedicated to Whiskey Rose.

I almost lost it then. It took ages for me to get over

it when Two went missing, and I spent thousands of dollars following every tip about where she might have gone in the city, only to discover that my psycho fan had her taxidermied like a stuffed animal. By then, Billie had adopted Three to come and live with us. We already didn't go anywhere without him. Though, technically, Three is mine—just like One and Two were—she is as attached to the void as I am, and after Two's disappearance, we weren't taking any chances on anything happening to him.

It got ten times worse after I saw the crime scene photos of Two. Ridgefield swore she died of natural causes, and I want to believe that.

Then again, he pulled a gun on me when he couldn't get my attention...

They had to lock Ridgefield up. He was too dangerous to be left out on his own, and I *knew* that... but in the blinding stage lights in Anaheim, when I thought I saw him, it didn't matter what I knew. I swore it was Ridgefield, and I *did* lose it.

I screamed. I screamed so damn loud that I burst something in my throat, and the concert came to a quick end right after that.

God fucking bless Billie. She was on the phone with the Department of Corrections at Rikers Island minutes after I was shuffled backstage. Trembling, gasping that I saw him, I saw *Ridgefield*, she did everything to prove that it was impossible.

Logically, I knew that. All of my venues have biometric scanning to keep out well-known nuisances; at my level of fame, I'd be a fool to think I only had *one* dangerous fan. We had metal detectors, too, so it's not like anyone could've brought in a gun. That asshole almost got me last summer because I was outside.

Now? Now I don't go outside anymore... and even though we got proof that Ridgefield is safely behind bars, that didn't change anything about what happened on that stage.

If anything, knowing that I imagined him made it *worse*.

You know the downside of being a superstar? You can't fucking pick your wedgie without some camera catching it. There are at least eight different 4k angles of Whiskey Rose losing her mind—and her voice—up online at this very moment, no matter how hard Charlotte tries to get them taken down.

My lawyer is worth every penny I pay her, but even she can't work miracles.

So, yeah. Even if I could go outside without my fans seeing me or some creep following me, I wouldn't if only because the scandal hasn't died down fast enough for me just yet. My team has explained away my absence from any sightings or interviews due to doctor-mandated 'vocal rest', but the truth is that I just don't want to face the media—or the world—right now.

But that doesn't mean that *Billie* has to be cooped up here with me, and once again I try to tell her that it's okay for her to take a single weekend off from Sierra duty.

She's curled up on the same plush settee with the magenta cushions as I am. I have my legs tucked beneath me, Three sprawled out on my lap. He's a longhaired void, rumbling softly as he sleeps, completely oblivious to the fact that Billie agreed to bring Three to the groomer before heading out this evening.

If she heads out…

"I don't know, Sierra. It seemed like a good idea when Trev invited me out to Connecticut for the weekend. Now I'm thinking I should cancel."

I raise my eyebrows at her. "I hope you're not doing it because you think you need to be on babysitting duty."

Billie isn't my blood, but she doesn't have to be. She's the closest thing to a sister I've ever had; after I was emancipated from my money-grubbing parents, she's the *only* family I have. Not just my manager, Billie is my best friend (apart from Three), and the only person in this world that I'd trust with our cat.

At thirty-three, she's two years older than I am, though I've known her since she was sixteen, I was fourteen, and we were part of a teenage girl group with Tandy Lewis. Thr33peat. Our popularity took off almost out of the gate, and though I always thought Billie's big, bouncy golden curls and bright blue eyes would've caught the public's eye, for some reason, I became America's sweetheart.

Whiskey fucking Rose.

I guess it worked out. By the time Thr33peat broke up for good when I was nineteen, Billie decided she was done with show business. Tandy could've hopped in the Hudson for all I cared after the way she betrayed me, but Billie... I always loved her. I looked up to her. And after she went to school for business management, I replaced my first manager with Billie.

We've been the dream team ever since.

Well, until Billie started dating Trevor Daniels more than a year ago, and I kind of became the third wheel...

Billie sighs. "I want to make sure you're okay."

"Yeah? And I want to make sure that you don't blow this thing you've got going with Trevor." No matter how awkward I feel about it. "He loves you. You dig him. You can't always be here watching me, B. Go. Enjoy the weekend. I'll find something to do."

"Sierra..."

Uh-oh. I know that tone. "What?"

Billie gives me a look. "Don't call Jared while I'm gone."

I'm an actress. Well, *now* I am. I'll always be a singer first, but with two films under my belt, there's no denying that I can slip into another role as easily as I've been Whiskey Rose all along.

When I got my first role, tabloids went nuts that I'd fail miserably. That my name—and, okay, my boobs—were the only reason the producers were willing to give me a shot. I sure as hell showed them. Music might be my first love, but you don't grow up in the business and survive as long as I have without being able to act your ass off.

In an instant, I'm so innocent, butter wouldn't melt in my mouth. "Call my ex? Why would I do that?"

Anyone else would've bought it.

Anyone else but Billie.

She snorts. "Maybe because you fall back on that tool whenever you're feeling horny? I understand having an itch you need scratched, but there's gotta be someone else. What about Greg? Or Nicholas? Ooh, how about Colin? Didn't you give him your personal number?"

I did, and then I blocked him when my co-star got a little too clingy.

"I'm not interested in Colin. And, no, I'm not interested in rekindling things with Jared, either. I'm just..." I exhale roughly, snagging the end of my braid, twirling the tail around my pointer finger. "*I'm bored.*"

That's true, but I'm also just a little jealous.

I want what Billie has with Trevor. I want a real relationship. I always have. It's just... I'm thirty-one now. After a lifetime in show biz, I've accepted that that's not in the cards for someone like me.

I've tried twice. The first time was with someone in the business. Jared Turner has a career trajectory just like mine. We both started out in our teens, members of same-sex singing groups; I was a member of Thr33-peat while he was the lead singer of Cool Guyz. It was inevitable that we'd hook up, and we did.

I fell hard, too. At sixteen, love seems so big. So all-consuming. He was my first everything. First kiss. First fuck. First love.

First heartbreak.

I loved Jared with everything I had, but I wasn't enough. When I was nineteen, I discovered he was cheating on me with Tandy, the other girl in Thr33peat. He claimed it was because I was too busy for him, spending all my time building the Whiskey Rose brand.

Fuck that. If he really loved me, he would've kept his dick in his pants.

On the plus side, Tandy's betrayal led to Thr33peat breaking up and Whiskey Rose finally taking off on her own. I released "Heart Barely Used" that year as my debut single, written with Jared in mind, and it's gone triple platinum since.

Billie's right, though. He *is* a tool—

"Hey. I've got an idea," my manager suddenly announces.

I'm sure she does. I might be looking for a distraction, but she knows me well enough to already have one in mind. "Lay it on me."

"I was just thinking, why don't you go through your fan mail?" Before I can groan, she hurriedly adds, "I had a couple of bags brought to the study the other day. You used to love going through it. That'll keep you busy if nothing else."

And though she doesn't add it, I know what else she's thinking: *and keeping you from calling Jared Turner.*

Yeah... sorry, Billie. Not likely.

But I know what I'm doing. Over the last twelve years, Jared has done everything he can think of to win me back. And while I've had my fun with him—as Billie loves to remind me—it's never that serious. I don't want my heart getting broken again.

Then, four years ago, I met a nice guy. Damon. He was an accountant. Liked to wear suits, and could've been a model if he had the arrogance for it. He was handsome and sweet, and I really felt like I could be Sierra around him.

We lasted a year before Patrick Ridgefield scared him off. I didn't know that at the time Damon dumped me, but that was another part of Patrick's eventual confession.

He threatened to lop off Damon's dick if he ever touched me again. And instead of telling me about it, Damon made up some ridiculous excuse and disappeared, leaving me easy prey for when Ridgefield finally attacked me.

Billie is super careful to shield me from the creeps out there. She has a team of social media pros who post for me and screen all my messages, offers, and emails. Whenever I get physical mail, she has it sorted and put through an x-ray machine before it ever reaches me, then even goes through the approved letters herself for suspicious ones.

Most fan letters are harmless. I've gotten some new obsessed fans that Roy's keeping an eye on, but my inner circle is very careful not to trigger me after the whole Patrick Ridgefield situation.

Maybe Billie's right. After California, I got a lot more messages than usual. Some were pissed because I had to cancel all of my tour dates through December, but others wanted to show their support for me during these trying times.

Reading letters from fans who adore Whiskey Rose might be what I need to remember why I enjoy my alter ego as much as I do. Because lately... I don't know.

I shrug. "I can do that."

She reaches out, patting my shoulder. "Trust me. You've got more than enough fan mail in the study to keep you busy through Monday. I'll be back then. Unless you changed your mind and want me to stay..."

"Nah. I mean it, B. Go out and have fun." No reason

why we both have to be alone. "Me and Three can survive without you until then."

"Don't forget. I'm running Three to the groomer to take care of a couple of those mats before I go. I'll stay with him the whole time, then bring him back myself before heading out with Trevor around…" Billie glances at her phone. "Six o'clock sound okay?" At my nod, she asks, "You want me to bring you some food back before I go?"

"I'll be fine. I know the delivery protocols by heart. If I get hungry, I'll order something in to the Dorado."

Billie nods, her curls bouncing as she climbs up off of the settee. She holds out her hands. "Here. Give me Three. I'll get him settled in with the carrier."

Better her than me. "I'd take him if I could."

"I know. And don't worry about it. I won't let him out of my sight."

I'm not the only one who was traumatized by what Ridgefield did. I have to remember that.

Giving Billie a smile, I pass Three over to her. "I trust you."

I need to be able to trust *someone*.

SIERRA

It's a little after four when Billie heads out, her rolling suitcase in one hand, a very grumpy Three in his carrier in the other.

Poor fella. I made the mistake once of trying to cut a dingleberry out of his fur when he was a kitten and, well, if he hadn't already been neutered when we adopted him, he might have been just then when my scissors accidentally slipped. From that moment on, I decided to leave grooming his fur to the pros no matter how ticked off that'll make my poor cat.

He'll stew about it when she brings him back for a little bit. I'll give him a few of his favorite treats. He'll get over it, and I'll have my snuggle partner for the weekend.

Unless... unless I can get a real guy to keep me company while Billie's with Trev.

When I'm on the road, I'm too busy to think about how long it's been since I've gotten any myself. Between touring, traveling, checking in and out of hotels, doing promo, pre-checks, meet and greets, then the show itself... I'm booked. Add in the fact that I'm also way too famous for one-night stands and I'm kind of screwed.

Or not, as it were.

I don't do roadies. Sorry, but I haven't met a road dog who knows the meaning of being 'discreet'. Buying their silence seems a little too close to paying for the deed to me. My security is definitely off-limits, and I'm usually so beat after a concert, all I want to do is unwind, then pass out.

That's the problem here. I've been put on house arrest—oh, *sorry*, vocal rest for the unforeseen future. Through Christmas at least, and since we're not even close to Thanksgiving yet, I don't know how much longer I can take being cooped up here.

Talk about a one-eighty. I filmed two movies last year, released an album, nearly got fucking *shot*, and launched two separate legs of my world tour. I've performed on six award shows, did countless interviews, and all of that I fit in by October.

Is it a surprise that I'm going stir-crazy? I haven't had this much time to myself since my stage momager decided to pull me from school when I was a kid, throwing me into everything from pageants to talent competitions to television auditions, just seeing what would stick.

I'm proficient in eight different types of dance, including polka. I've done community theater and sketch comedy shows for the local upstate channels. I was a pretty decent gymnast until I gave up those lessons for my voice teacher.

Singing is where I found my spot. My place where I belonged. For almost twenty years, it's been my life now, and—usually—I don't regret a minute of what I sacrificed to get here... until just finding a guy to, as Billie put it, 'scratch my itch' becomes a damn production.

Now, there's no way I could ever draw Damon back into the fucked-up world of being Whiskey Rose's normie boyfriend, whether I forgave him or not. And no matter how many times Jared has sworn he's changed, I'd be an idiot if I gave him another chance.

But he's in the same type of life. He knows the risks, and the rewards. It won't be a relationship starter, but fuck if I don't need to get laid.

No. I shouldn't do it. I shouldn't—

Oh. I'm sitting on the settee and my phone's in my hand. How did it get there?

Well, since I'm already swiping my message app open...

Hey. Wyd? Are you in town?

There. Jared will know exactly why I'm texting him, and if he's not out doing some promo for his upcoming album, he might be in the city. Like me, his home base is in Manhattan. Unless he's busy, he won't turn down an open invitation from Whiskey Rose.

I'm dying for a distraction almost as much as I am some dick. Cabin fever has firmly set in, and since I'm feeling more like myself—like Sierra—than I have in ages, maybe a booty call with Jared Turner is just what I need.

The first week after my meltdown, I honestly needed the downtime. I had nightmares of Patrick Ridgefield sneaking out of Rikers, finding his way to the Upper West Side, and pointing his gun in my face again. The scream that 'broke my voice' really did rupture something, and there was a reason why Dr. Martin put me on 'vocal rest'.

My doctor team was afraid that I'd developed vocal nodules over the years. I've been singing my entire life, and though my signature rasp is something I was born with, the way my voice cracked onstage before I screamed was something altogether new.

Thankfully, it wasn't a nodule. Nodules come about after long-term, repetitive misuse of your voice. I'd be a fucking fool to mess around with my moneymaker, no matter how much I'm starting to feel the strain of a lifetime lived for the public.

It wasn't a nodule—but it was a polyp. That single scream did enough damage that I wasn't allowed to use my voice at all for two weeks. I couldn't, either. It hurt too much, and that was when I wasn't struggling with the sensation that something was stuck in my throat.

By Tuesday of this week, I was feeling a little better. For most of the day, I was quiet, only talking to Billie and Roy. If Jared decides to come over, I won't need to do any talking... though I will have to be careful not to scream, just in case.

I stare at my phone, willing him to answer.

Ten minutes. I give him ten minutes after the text goes from 'delivered' to 'read' without a response before I stick my phone into the pocket of my leggings and get up from the settee.

Fan mail, huh? In the study?

Why not?

BILLIE TOLD ME SHE LEFT A COUPLE OF BAGS OF FAN MAIL for me to dig through. We need to work on her definition of 'couple' because, holy shit, there are *nine* in here. And they're not small bags, either. These suckers are huge. I'm 5'7", and I could probably climb inside of one and have it reach up to my boobs!

Okay. I admit, I haven't done this in... a while. Usually, one of the social media team members goes through the letters, sending out a recent headshot of me with a printed signature on it if the letter calls for a kind of response. Every now and then, they'll find a couple of real touching messages and pass them along to me, but I never really have the time to do this.

When I knock over the first bag, letting the letters, packages, and manila envelopes slide on the floor like an avalanche, I suddenly remember why.

With Three at the groomers, this is probably the best time to do this. My cat would probably skate around on the mail or use the post office bag as a cat bed instead of the many I have tucked around the apartment for him.

An hour into reading a good chunk of the first pile I made, I'm feeling a lot better about being Whiskey Rose. When I'm not 'on', it's easy to forget just how much she means—*I* mean—to so many people. These letters are a connection to my most engaged fans, and I actually set aside a few that I plan on answering personally.

Once I clear out that stack, I grab the bag, dragging it closer to me. Instead of sitting at the desk that Billie uses when we're at the Dorado, I got comfy, straddling my legs while dropping more mail in between the gap. I move the bag there so I can dump it out, pausing when something seems to actually drag with the thick plastic.

I grab it with one hand, hefting it up and down a couple of times. Unless I'm imagining it, there's something that's kind of heavy-ish toward the bottom. Definitely heavier than a regular-old envelope.

Huh.

Hoping I don't suffocate, I basically dive in. It's probably not the smartest idea to pull the bag part way over my head—and I can just see the headlines now: *pop star asphyxiates herself with mailbag*—but, suddenly, I'm determined to see what it is.

My fingers brush against a cardboard side. A box? Package, maybe.

Ooh... what if it's a present?

I wrap my fingers around it. Since I can, I estimate it's about three or four inches high. It's definitely heavy, and I grunt a little as I yank it out.

Look at that. It *is* a package.

Shifting it so that I can read the address label, my heart skips a beat.

Why? Because it's addressed to *me*. And I don't mean Whiskey Rose. I mean *me*:

Sierra Landry
℅ Bickles Management
Dorado Apartments

Now, it's not so unusual that a fan would know my name. When I was in Thr33peat, when I wasn't known as 'Three', I was still Sierra. Whiskey Rose didn't become a thing until I got my first tattoo as an F-U to my mom after I was emancipated. The rose on my side, near my midriff, was shown off when I did the photoshoot for my first magazine cover. A new life needed a new name, and I was christened Whiskey Rose by the perv who took the shots before trying to convince me to go home with him.

I went home with Jared Turner instead—who was seventeen, blond, and undeniably delicious—and history was made in more than one way that day.

That was fifteen years ago, though. Calling me Sierra would be like addressing Lady Gaga as Stefani. You know Gaga isn't her real name, but she *is* Gaga, just like I'm Whiskey Rose.

I tap my fingernail against the USPS priority mail box.

For Sierra, huh?

Color me intrigued.

It has to be safe to open. Billie would never let a package through that might have a bomb in it or something else that might hurt me. Clinging to that belief, I set the box down and climb up, searching her desk for a pair of scissors to get the box open.

And when I finally do? I'm a little surprised by what I find.

It's a book. And a weird one, too.

It's pretty big. A little larger than a standard hardcover, it's bound in leather. There's a pentagram embossed on the front in gold, and when I ease the cover open, the title page reveals that it's called the *Grimoire du Sombra*.

What the fuck does that mean?

I don't know. It's gotta be an old book. The pages are yellowed, the print looking more like old-fashioned typing instead of an actual modern-day printer. It has that old book smell to it, plus... smoke? Weird, but it kind of smells like smoke.

Maybe it belonged to a cigarette smoker in the past. Glancing at the inner cover, I see that there's a list of four previous owners written inside.

Susanna Benoit

AMY

Shannon Crewes

Kennedy Barnes

The first one is done in pen. The second? I kid you not, it's crayon. The last two look like they were scrawled in charcoal to the point that there's a ghost of a smudge left behind on the title page.

It looks valuable. The names probably bring down its worth, but it's still cool to see.

I just don't know why this was sent to me.

Before I set it aside, I use my thumb to flip through the pages. They're brittle yet surprisingly sturdy, and I don't tear any of them. As the pages fly by, I'm even more puzzled why this was sent to me. Apart from the word 'grimoire' in the title, nothing else is in English. I mean, I recognize the alphabet in here, but I have no idea what language it's written in.

And that's pretty weird, too, since I've been all over the world. I might not be able to speak more than English, some passable Spanish, and a couple of important phrases in Mandarin, Hindi, and Italian, but I don't know what any of this says.

Until I slow down my flipping just in time to see some cursive written in the margin on one particular page.

Someone has written the word 'manifest' next to the first paragraph on the page. The second half has a star next to it, plus the word 'promise'. Hmm. Interesting. So are the instructions above them, explaining how to create a... hang on.

A protective circle?

Draw this symbol in yellow chalk, then create a circle out of salt around it...

What the hell is this?

My gaze darts to the center of the page. The print is bolded: **VERUS AMOR**. In the same script, someone has written two words in English.

True love.

I blink, making sure I read that right. I did, and I look at the symbol again. I didn't notice before, but it's a pentagram, just like what's embossed on the cover of the *Grimoire du Sombra.*

A grimoire... isn't that, like, a spell book?

Is this a spell?

A true love spell?

Holy shit. That would be fucking amazing!

Oh my God, I've got to try that.

Can you imagine? No dating. No wasting your time, trying to find the right guy. What if I could read some strange words and *poof*! Here's my true love, and I won't have to share him with the rest of the world because he's mine.

Do I honestly believe this will work? No. Not really. But if it did... let's just say, I think it might be worth scrounging up some yellow chalk and salt and giving this a try.

Now, where can I get my hands on some yellow chalk and salt?

BILLIE IS STILL AT THE GROOMERS, WAITING FOR THREE to finish up. She's kept me posted with updates—including the amount of blood our grumpy cat drew from Mandy when she tried to clip his claws—and I can tell she's going to be occupied a little longer.

And that's why I text Roy to see if he can bring me what I need to delve into my witchy side.

If Billie's my sister, Roy Saunders is the father figure I wish I had when I was younger. He's also my head of security and has been since he was hired by the record label to watch over Thr33peat. Though he's pushing sixty now, and a lot of the muscle he carried fifteen years ago is turning a little more solid these days, he's only the second person I trust in this world.

On my bad nights, or when the fans and the paps won't be run off by the Dorado's security team, he stays over in the spare guest room. But because he also has his own life—including his sweet wife, Dawn, who is gracious enough to share Roy with me and Billie, as well as two daughters a little younger than me—he takes as much downtime as possible to spend with his family when we're in town.

Luckily, Dawn's out with Sam and Tina, seeing a Friday night flick in midtown. Roy's only a quick subway ride away from the Dorado, and the only reason why I ask him instead of getting someone to deliver it to me is because I'm sure he wants the excuse to check in on me and Billie.

We haven't seen him in person since Monday, though he texts every night to make sure we're doing okay. This is as much a forced vacation for my security team as it is me since I'm relying on the Dorado to keep me safe right now.

Roy doesn't argue because, at the end of the day, I'm the boss. Well, Billie is, but that's because she always does what's best for me.

And that's how I end up with my head of security handing me a bag from Duane Reade. Only after he's standing in the gallery with me do I realize that I should've asked him to pick up some take-out for me on his way.

Oh, well. Maybe later.

"You got the salt?" I take the bag, peeking inside. "I see the chalk. Is it yellow? It looks white."

"I had to go to two stores to find yellow chalk, Sierra," Roy says, patient as ever. "I got it, though."

"Thanks, Roy. You're the best."

When he was younger, Roy had dark brown hair. These days, it's more salt than pepper as he runs his thick fingers through it. "Anything for one of my girls. But I gotta ask... why exactly do you need a pack of yellow chalk?"

Good question.

Do I really want to tell my head of security that I'm entertaining myself by playing with magic?

In answer, I grimace and tap my throat.

Roy's curious expression softens. "Forget I asked. How's your throat? Feeling better?"

I'm going to fucking Hell, aren't I?

I don't whisper, not really, because that can lead to more stress on my vocal cords. Instead, I do my best to speak softly. "I'm doing okay. I was reading an article that says gargling with salt water might be good for my polyp. I'm gonna try, then turn in early."

He nods. And though I'm one hundred percent convinced he's dying to ask me about the chalk again, he squeezes my shoulder. "You know I'm always on duty. You need something, you tell me. 'Kay, kid?"

I nod right back at him, keeping a faint smile in place as he tells me good night, then heads to the elevator.

Only once he's gone do I grab the bag and haul ass toward my bedroom.

Just in case Billie decides to chat some more when she drops Three off tonight, I'd rather not have her walk in on me trying to cast a spell I found in an old book. I'm pretty sure she's already concerned about my mental health. Watching me draw a pentagram on my hardwood floor with the yellow chalk before doing my best to create a circle with the container of salt... she'll have Dr. Lopez in for an emergency therapy session before I can blink.

No. She deserves this weekend away with Trev. I've never seen her so happy as when she's with him, and I know that she's only been pulling away from him lately because she has her own commitment issues.

Kind of like how, oh, Billie refuses to settle down with anyone...

Trevor's been good for her. He reminds her there's

more to life than just being Whiskey Rose's manager. She needs that.

Just like I need to forget I'm Whiskey Rose sometimes.

I have yellow chalk residue and grains of salt all over my hands by the time I'm done. Wiping them on my thigh so that I don't mess up the old book any more than someone already has, I heft it up in my arms and begin to read the 'manifest' part of the spell.

Woof. That is not fun. Each word is more difficult to pronounce than the last, and I get the idea that I'm probably fucking this up anyway since I have no clue what I'm reading.

By the time I finish stumbling over the first paragraph, there's no chance in hell that I'm going to attempt the second part. Especially since the whole idea of making a 'promise' when I don't know what I'm saying rubs me the wrong way.

Hey. Sometimes it feels like I cut my baby teeth on contracts. If my mom taught me anything, it's that I should always read every line before I sign my life away.

Trust me. After she stole all of the money I made during my time in Thr33peat, I learned that lesson all the way to my soul.

Besides, if this spell does what I'm guessing it's supposed to, there's no reason to 'promise' anything.

Let me just 'manifest' my true love in that circle I set up and see what shakes out from there.

Let's go.

I'm ready.

I wait—and... nothing happens.

Huh.

Well, that's a letdown. Even more annoyingly, I drew the pentagram with chalk, then poured the salt on my *bedroom* floor. Unless I want to walk through it and track it all over the apartment later, I'm going to have to clean that up soon.

We have a housekeeper. We have a housesitter, too, for when we're on the road. Since Billie and I have been staying at the Dorado for a while, both Gladys and Maurice have been given a paid-for vacation until the new year. It seemed like a good idea at the time, especially since Billie insisted on privacy during my recovery, but now cleaning that mess is up to me.

And I didn't even get a true love out of it.

Ugh. I guess I should go see where Gladys keeps the cleaning supplies.

Here's hoping it's in the kitchen somewhere; otherwise I might just have to text Roy again.

DAGON

The duke's mate is once again sitting along the fountain, head tipped back as she glances up at the blue sky.

When I first came to serve Susanna as her personal guard, I had never seen this color before. In Caol, everything is in shades of reds, blacks, browns, and grays. I knew orange from the fire pits, gold from the craftsman's eyes, and green from the soldiers that patrolled our village, making sure we followed every one of Duke Haures's decrees.

I am not as young as some of the demons in my former village, and at five centuries, I wasn't an elder, either. I was still a mature male and one of the lead hunters for my clan. So long as I provided meat to barter, I was left to my lair and the shadows. I had no dealings with the green-eyed soldiers until I pledged myself to the mortal woman as her second shadow.

The duke? I was too insignificant to know much of the ruler of Sombra—until I discovered that he was the fated mate of the queer human woman that saved me from the shadows... *twice*.

The capital of Sombra is called Mavro. It is an oasis tucked in the center of our fire-filled, shadowy realm, and much cooler far from the ash fields. There is no ash here; everything is tinged with blue. I didn't understand why, and then I was tossed to my knees in front of Duke Haures more than three decades ago.

Legends told that our ruler is different than the other Sombra demons. The legends are true. Instead of red skin, he is colorless. My hair is like that of the deepest shadows on the edge of our realm. His is the same bright shade as his fangs, plus the tusks he has.

And his eyes...

Duke Haures has eyes the same color as the rest of Mavro, and I know that's why Susanna stares up at the first moon like this.

Though the duke adores his mate, he is protective of her. He hides her in the palace, careful to keep her existence a secret from the rest of the realm. He does so for the same reason why he showed me mercy for trying to call his mate mine: because, as his mate, she is in danger. Any demon who wants to strike at the duke would find no better a target than the tiny female covered all in white, marking her as Duke Haures's one true mate.

So he hides her, and when I explained that I didn't lust for her—because as devoted as I am to seeing her safe, she is *not* my mate—but that I owed her my life, Duke Haures granted me permission to watch over her when he couldn't.

Like this moment.

Two clan leaders from rival villages have petitioned Duke Haures to hear their squabbles. Neither knows of Susanna's existence, so he asked her to leave the throne room, commanding me to follow behind her.

I don't need to be commanded. Until I have my own mate to shadow, I will be there for Susanna whenever she needs me.

Three decades ago, she was the strange creature who challenged an arkoda to give me time to survive its attack. For years, she was my quiet mistress, both of us unsure what kind of relationship was respectable between a poor hunter and the duke's mate. But once she also understood I served her because I owed her a life debt—for saving me from the arkoda, then when the duke called for my horns—and that there's nothing that I want from her but to square that debt, she became my friend.

I approach her now as such.

She's the one who insists I call her Susanna. Truth

be told, she is the Duchess of Sombra, but only the duke uses that title when he wants to make a point in front of the few demons who know of her existence. Other than that, she is his beloved mate—and to those of us who have learned what a sweet yet formidable female she is, she is simply Susanna.

Gazing up at the moon, I know she's thinking of her mate. Though she is not a demoness, I've learned through the decades that human females love as fiercely as we demons do. When she cannot be with Duke Haures, she's counting down the moments until she can.

Just like I've been counting down the moments until the gods take pity on me and put my female in my path...

I don't know if they will. Being Susanna's guard means that I rarely leave Mavro. My mate would have to cross my path at the palace for me to recognize her or somehow call me to her so that I know she's mine.

When I peer over at Susanna, I wonder if that is what the gods have in store for me. She came from the legendary world of humans on the other side of the veil. After bonding with Duke Haures, she chose to stay in Sombra. The first time I saw her, I was so surprised by the sight of her that I thought she was just another horror to come from the shadows on the edge of Sombra.

She managed to defeat the most brutal beast with

nothing more than her wits. Instead of being a horror, she admitted she was a human, and she saved me because it never occurred to her not to.

She saved me from the arkoda, and until the moment I have a mate of my own to protect, I owe my entire existence to this female.

But when I look at her, I can't help but sense that the gods put her in my path for another reason. Not just to save me, but because I, too, am meant to bond with one of the mortal females in another world.

I could only be so fortunate. At least, if I do, I will know better than to insult my mate by pointing out her rounded ears or flat teeth like I did my first meeting with Susanna. If she hadn't taken pity on me, asking her mate to spare me a return trip to the depths of the shadows after I insulted her, then triggered his jealousy... I wouldn't be here to hope for a mate.

But I do.

A mate of my own... that's all I long for.

And when Duke Haures strides out into the garden, Susanna's head twisting in time to see him approaching her, I'm reminded again how desperately I want a female to look at me with such an expression of love.

Ah, but that is not my fate, I think, slipping into the shadows so that I can leave the duke and his mate to their privacy.

It's not my fate... at least, not yet.

Another moon. Another meeting that Duke Haures cannot avoid.

I don't know what the stories outside of Mavro tell of these most recent cycles. If the other Sombrans whisper that the duke—after more than two millennia—found his mate. I know it was a surprise to me when I chanced upon Susanna, and that was within days of her arrival in Sombra. It's been decades since then, and still he hides her.

During the time of the gold moon, he's even more protective of her. Though they've chosen not to have spawn until the entire realm accepts her as their ruler's mate, Duke Haures and Susanna disappear into their private quarters in the days leading up to and after the gold moon rises high in the sky.

They mate. I would never admit it to anyone, but I've seen them touching each other from a distance when they were together in the gardens, and my given lair is near enough to their quarters that I've heard the sounds they make.

I have never mated before. I've spent my five centuries waiting for my one true mate to recognize me as hers. Accidentally seeing the duke bowing his large body over Susanna's much smaller one, feeding his cock into her cunt... I'm not jealous of him. At least, not because it is Susanna who takes him, or because I don't get to mate her.

I am jealous because I want my female, and my fist is a poor substitute for the one female meant for me.

I ache for her more during the gold moon than any other part of the cycle, and I'm grateful that another one is behind me.

But because the gold moon is over and the bonded demons of Sombra aren't distracted by their need to claim their mates again and again, plenty of villagers have come to Mavro to meet with the duke.

And that means that Susanna and I are once again in her favorite garden.

The water in the fountain tinkles softly. Even from my post, I can scent the flowers in bloom that grow at her feet. Susanna has a book on her lap, though she isn't reading it. Instead, she's plucked a flower with petals as blue as the rest of Mavro, twirling the stem between her fingers.

And that's when I suddenly stumble forward, nearly falling to the cobblestones that create the path between the palace and the fountain.

Susanna glances up. It took a long time for me to not show my surprise at how dark and dim her human eyes are, set deep in her strangely pale face. I've grown to appreciate the human's strange beauty, though I don't lust after her. I never have. Duke Haures would eliminate me if I did, and should he spare me, I would do it myself.

I don't know my mate yet, but even then I will not betray her.

The stumble is unexpected. It feels as though someone had speared me through the back, knocking me forward. With another tug, it yanks on me, trying to drag me away.

No. I'm strong enough to resist it. Bracing my solid feet against the hard ground, I dig in with the claws on my toes to keep the invisible tether from moving me more than a few inches away from where I nearly fell.

Whatever strange magic is at work on me, I resist it... but when my body begins to stir, my cock coming to life beneath the shadow-woven coverings I wear when I'm in Susanna's sight... I can't stop it from readying itself to fuck.

I only get hard when I think of my mate. Otherwise my cock lays limp along my thigh, useful only to relieve myself in the toilet. I'm careful not to ever think lusty thoughts when I'm on duty in case Susanna—or Duke Haures—gets the wrong idea.

Now? I don't know what is happening to me, only that it's completely out of my control.

Another tug, and I gasp. My cock twitches, pushing against the shadows. I quickly conjure more so that it's not so noticeable. In response, it feels even hotter and heavier—and eager to sink into somewhere warm and welcoming.

Mate...

Is that what it is? This feeling that I'm being pulled somewhere else... is it my mate?

Susanna sets aside her book. Her flower hangs limply between her fingers as she rises to her feet. "Dagon? Are you alright?"

I... might be. "Susanna." Her name is a rumble as I twist my hips, trying to hide my reaction from her. "Something is calling me."

Her lips part. "*Verus amor*? Could it be?"

Verus amor... the matefinder spell that first brought Susanna to Sombra.

"I don't know," I admit. "Something has taken a hold of me. Like it wants me to follow it somewhere."

Like it wants me to mate it when I do...

"Haures told me the spell got him in the middle of a meeting and he had no choice but to go. Does it feel like that?"

"Aye. Yes, I think so."

"Then what are you still doing here?" She waves her hands at me. "I know how much you've been waiting for your mate. Go to her, Dagon. Right now, she's waiting for *you*."

I only hope that is true.

But... "Who will watch over you?"

"Me?" Her laugh is a tinkling sound. "Don't you worry about me."

"Susanna—"

"I mean it, Dagon. Don't you remember your promise?"

I do. When Susanna saved my life, I pledged it to her. Of course, being the kind female she is, she tried to absolve me of my promise, but I was as stubborn three decades ago as I am now. I insisted, and she only agreed to allow me to repay my life debt to her until I saved her from a near-fatal accident or I needed to be free to pledge myself to my one true mate.

Susanna is immortal now. She has been since she bonded with Duke Haures. It would take more to save her than even I can do, so we both agreed I would guard her when her mate couldn't until the moment I found mine.

Is that now?

Am I afraid that it isn't?

It doesn't matter. Susanna is right. Some sort of magic is calling me, and I'd be a coward if I refused to answer.

I am Dagon. I am a fierce hunter from Caol. I am no coward.

"I will claim her," I promise, making another heartfelt vow, "and once my female is my bonded mate, I will bring her to meet the female who saved her male."

Susanna's cheeks pinken. "You don't have to do

that. Just knowing that you won't be lonely any longer is enough for me, old friend."

She's right. I've been lonely for a long, long time, and if what I suspect is true, that might finally come to an end this eve.

I bow my head in respect to the duchess. "Thank you, my lady."

She waves her flower at me. "Good luck!"

THE LAST VISION I HAVE OF SOMBRA IS SUSANNA holding the blue-petaled flower, smiling at me as I allow the magic to lift me off of my feet. The moment I do, a large, deep portal made of shadows and flame erupts at my back. The magic twists me in time so that I can face it before it swallows me whole.

Seconds later, it spits me out onto a floor made of wood. A tantalizing scent filters in through my nostrils, heading straight to my cock.

It weeps, and I groan, every instinct inside of me crying out to find the source of it.

Mate, my heart sings. *Mate.*

I landed in a crouch. Rising up, I don't pay any attention to my surroundings past seeing that I am alone. My mate is not here.

I shall find her.

It takes one step. One step forward, prepared to use

my hunting skills to track down my mate before I slam face-first into an invisible barrier in front of me. Throwing my hands out, ignoring the ache in my cock and my nose, I turn, testing the space around me. I go a full circle before realizing something very significant.

I'm *trapped*.

And that's when I glance at the wooden ground beneath my solid feet and see the protective sigil below me. It's etched with giz, then circle of salt surrounds it. In an instant, I understand that my mate *did* summon me, and she knows enough to expect that her true love —her *verus amor*—is a demon.

It's only fair since I now know for sure that my mate is one of the legendary humans like Susanna.

CHAPTER 4
LASER POINTERS

SIERRA

The best I can find is a spray bottle full of window cleaner.

Hoping that will work to clean up the salt and the chalk, I snag that and one of the dish towels I found piled up under the kitchen sink. I kick the cabinet door closed with my foot before glancing around the pristine kitchen.

The table is empty. All of the lights are off in here since Gladys is on vacation. It's probably the cleanest room in the whole apartment right now 'cause God knows that me and Billie rarely use it for its purpose.

Ask us to choreograph a dance in an hour? You got it. Tell us to prepare a song in half that time? We'll look like we've rehearsed for a week. Take Billie's phone and quiz her on my upcoming schedule, she'll get every damn detail right, down to my three-minute pee breaks.

But plop either of us in front of a stove and expect something edible to come out? Yeah… that's not gonna happen.

That reminds me. I haven't had anything to munch on since she ran down to Charlie's Deli to grab us lunch. I'm not starving, though I can eat, and I know better than to go too long without food in case I screw up my metabolism.

I glance down at the window cleaner. If I order dinner on my phone, I should be able to clean up my mess before the delivery person makes it to the Dorado. Whoever they are, they'll have to drop it off at the front desk. One of the concierges who man it will let me know it's arrived, then bring it up for me.

It's such a hassle. Sometimes I wish I could just grab my phone, grab my wallet, and dash out for my own food. Billie does all the time, though she gets recognized plenty from her time as 'Two' in Thr33peat. When our old fans recognize her, though, it's as simple as a selfie, maybe an autograph, and a quick wave before she's on her way.

If Whiskey Rose decided to take a stroll down the street, there'd be a fucking *riot*.

Disguises used to help. I'd throw on a wig, some shades, and baggy clothes to hide the rest of my body.

With Roy walking nearby, we'd look like a dad and his daughter out for a stroll, and no one ever noticed it was me... until Roy got a bit of a fan club of his own, and I realized I could either replace Roy as my head of security or give up on even more of my freedom.

Nowadays, I accept that anywhere I go, I'll draw a crowd. Before the Ridgefield incident, I didn't care. I love my fans. I love meeting them, taking pics, talking to them. They've always been so good to me, supporting me no matter where my career takes me, and though some of them can be a little... extreme, I never thought I was in danger.

I know better now. Drawing a crowd? Not a good idea. Especially after what happened in California, it's just better if I lay low for a while.

Okay. Order food, clean up the chalk. I'm feeling like a burger tonight. If there's one bonus to having some downtime, it's getting to eat some of my favorite foods. I don't do that when I'm on tour, and I'm sure I'll regret double gym time in January, but for now? I might as well enjoy myself.

It's a good plan. A sound plan. Who knows? Maybe after I did that, I'd flip through that book some more, see what other 'spells' it has inside. If it wasn't for Billie being busy with Three, I'd call her up and tell her all about the *verus amor* spell and how ridiculous it was that I believed it could actually work.

Maybe later. Probably on Monday since she plans

on bringing Three home, leaving him with me in the apartment while she takes the drive out of the city to Connecticut with Trev.

Huh... I would've expected her back by now. It's almost six, after all, and as fluffy as Three is, it usually doesn't take this long for his grooming appointments. Honestly, if I didn't know better, I'd think Billie was stalling so she could get out of her weekend away with Trevor.

Nah. She wouldn't do that. Besides, she already told him she was going. If there's one thing I know about my best friend, once she gives her word, she almost never breaks it.

I hope she enjoys herself. And when I see her again, I'm sure she'll shake those golden curls of hers as she rolls eyes to hear what Sierra was up to while she was gone.

Hey. I'm sure she's used to it by now.

I LEFT THE DOOR TO MY BEDROOM OPEN SINCE NO ONE else was home. Swinging the window cleaner in one hand, flapping the dish towel absently with the other, I hum the melody for a new song I've been noodling on as I walk into my room.

The first thing I notice is that it's warm in here. Weird. It's November in Manhattan, and though it's technically still fall, the Dorado has the heat cranked so high, it's not unusual for me to walk around in shorts since I'm not leaving. I'm used to warm.

This isn't just warm. This is *hot*.

I choke. It's hot, but it also has this terrible smell. And, yes, living in Manhattan full-time means I've had to get used to some awful smells, even on the Upper West Side. This is... I don't know. Like rotten eggs mixed with barbecue.

Phew. I try to blow the stink out of my nose. My security team would have a conniption if I threw open my bedroom window, but it's rough. I might just have to leave the window cleaner and the rag in here, grab my phone, and hope the ventilation in the system takes care of the odor while I hang out in the living room.

That's the plan.

It doesn't happen quite like that.

I'll never know what it was that snagged my attention—or why I was so oblivious in the first place that I missed the big, hulking beast lurking in the middle of the circle of salt I spilled. Most likely because he was so dark, at first I didn't even notice him in the evening shadows.

I'd turned the light off when I left the room before. The heat and the stink slapped me in the face so suddenly, I didn't bother turning it back on since I was planning on grabbing my phone and backing right out of the room again to escape the uncomfortable space.

But something has me glancing to my side. Two red lights, thicker than laser pointers but just as bright, are floating near the circle of salt. Not on the floor, though. I actually have to tilt my head back a little to see them.

Below the lights, the shadows look impossibly dark. And, unless I'm imagining things, they're moving.

What the—

I move toward the nearest light switch and slap it. The light turns on, but the shadows don't vanish.

In fact, they become more noticeable beneath one of my overhead lights.

Because those shadows... they're part of a person—

No.

Creature.

That's what it is. I can't put it any nicer. It's a shadow creature... monster... *thing.*

I stop.

I stare.

It's fucking huge. Wide, too. But once I'm looking at it, I can make out a shape in the dark shadows. I see shoulders. Hair. Can't miss the horns that look like a goddamn bull, or how they jut out of head that's, like, two feet higher than mine.

Those glowing red dots? They're *eyes.*

Claws. Yup. Can't forget the claws that tip its long, thick fingers. Each point is at least three inches longer. One swipe and that thing could rip me the fuck open.

Holy... holy shit.

I almost throw up.

Seriously. The sudden terror rising up inside of me to see that there is a massive creature prowling around the inside of the circle of salt has my heart lodged in my throat. I can't even scream, and not because I'm thinking about my vocal cord injury.

I can't scream because fear has stolen my ability to make any other sound than a soft moan.

"Oh, God. What the... oh my *God*."

I back up. Why I don't run right out the door, I'll never know. The monster is in front of me, but I scoot all the way against the far wall as if some instinct is warning me to guard my back.

It's watching me, big body shifting so that he can train those glowing red eyes on me.

I've never felt more like prey in my life than I do at this moment. Staring down the barrel of Ridgefield's gun is a close second, but that prick was at least human.

This thing... isn't.

On the plus side, it doesn't look like it can escape the circle of salt on the floor. The way it's basically vibrating in place, moving around the space, I get the idea that if it could, it would be coming right for me.

And I brought this monster here.

I had to have. I highly doubt it's one hell of a coincidence that I get a strange book—a strange *spellbook*—

sent to me, I foolishly read one of the pages all because it had some English scrawled in the margins, and after I make a quick pit stop in the kitchen, I come back to my room to find this shadow creature waiting for me inside of the circle I put down.

Protective circle. The instructions told me the yellow chalk and the salt were for a protective circle.

Good. I'm thinking I need all the protection from that monster that I can get.

But, just in case...

My head swivels to my left. Crap. I forgot that the door to my bedroom is still open. I didn't close it behind me after I walked through the study and into my room.

Shit.

Now, I treasure my privacy. I lost so much of it during my younger years that I go to great lengths to have time on my own. Whether it's being snuck into the back of whatever hotel I'm staying at and immediately tossing the 'do not disturb' sign on the handle or blocking myself off from the rest of the apartment, anyone in my inner circle knows that an open door is an invitation.

A closed door? Means go the fuck away.

Billie could be dropping Three off any minute. Roy left after getting me the chalk and salt, but what if he decides to turn around and check in on me one last time before heading home to his wife and kids?

Nope. Gotta close the door—even if that means getting closer to the shadow monster.

Please, please, please let that circle hold.

It's watching me intently as I make my first move. With those peepers like traffic lights, I'd know if it blinked. It hasn't yet, and no, that's not creepy at all, is it?

Though I get the idea the monster can't leave the protective circle, I'm not taking any chances. With my back against the wall, I scoot all the way around the room until I reach my bedroom door. Using my toe, I kick it shut. A quick turn of the lock and no one will burst in on me while I deal with that thing I accidentally summoned.

Okay. I realize too late that I made a mistake in my fright. I locked the door—but I locked myself in the room with that thing!

What was I thinking? I mean, clearly, I'm *not*, but why didn't I bolt out the door while I had the chance?

C'mon, Sierra. This is Ridgefield all over again. When he whipped out that weapon, pointing it at me, any sense of self-preservation I thought I might have disappeared in the blink of an eye. I stood there, motionless, as the rest of the world reacted around me.

At least, this time, I moved. I reacted. It was quite probably the stupidest reaction I could make—and if this was my character Faye from the horror movie I have coming out next fall, I'd call her TSTL—but... I don't know. It seemed like the right idea at the time.

I'm saving Billie. I'm saving Three.

Did I sacrifice myself in the meantime?

I fucking hope not.

What do I do now? Maybe it's better if I stay in here because then it won't surprise me again. I can keep my eye on it while figuring out my next move.

Do I call Billie? Fuck, I *always* call Billie. No. Just in case that thing is dangerous, I'm not gonna get my best friend eaten by a shadow monster because I fooled around with a spellbook.

Roy? He should've been my first instinct, but he has a family. Can you imagine having to tell Dawn and the girls that I fed their father to a monster? Hell, no. Roy is trained for stalkers and aggressive fans, not monsters with *horns*.

Oh, God. Oh, no.

Oh, no, no, no...

The monster is still in the circle. Thank God I followed the instructions in the book because I can't imagine what it would've done if it got those massive claws it has on me.

I'm safe, for now. And the monster... it just cleared its throat.

It has a throat?

It must because, to my shock, it clears it, then actually *says* something out loud.

"Dagon."

So, uh, it's a *he*. That much is obvious now. That rumbling masculine voice he has... I don't know if shadow monsters have a gender, but I definitely think this one's a guy, even if I have no idea what he just said.

Dag-on? What?

He knows I'm clueless, too, and tries again. "Dagon *mate*."

I blink. Did he just say 'mate'?

No. It has to be something else. Some unintelligible noise that's definitely not a word for two animals fucking.

Right? Holy shit. I'm freaking out, so past gone that instead of melting down like I did in California, I'm almost numb to this situation. Because the monster is watching me so closely, I don't know what the hell he wants—or what I'm supposed to do.

I gape at him wordlessly.

He shows me his fangs.

They're the only spot of white out of a mass of darkness. They stand out because of that, curving over what I assume must be his lower lip. The fangs are that long. Pointed, too, like a carnivore.

A meat eater.

And, welp, I'm meat.

Oh. Okay.

I know *exactly* what to do.

I scream bloody murder.

DAGON

My mate is as skittish as she is gorgeous.

As she tiptoes closer to me, keeping me in her sight as though she expects me to go fully demonic and rush her, I admit she will be my greatest challenge as a hunter.

Why? Because she is also the most wary of prey.

I fear it won't be as easy to claim her as I believed it would be when I dreamed of a demoness female joining me in my lair, but though she is small and human just like Susanna is, she is mine.

Therefore she is *perfect*.

It is I who must change the way I approach her, I think as I watch her closely, trying to impress her with my strength, size, the darkness of my shadows, and the glow of my hunter's blood-red gaze. This is the most important hunt of my existence because, if I can snare my mate, I will want for nothing else. For five long centuries, she is all I desired.

And she is here.

When the duke is busy and she is lonely, Susanna has often relived her first meeting with Duke Haures to me. Not knowing that Sombra existed on the other side of the veil, she was surprised—and, yes, *frightened* —by his notably demon features. He is so much larger than she is, his ears pointier, his fangs sharper. He is a fierce ruler and her devoted mate, but she didn't know that at their initial encounter.

Strangely enough, my mate was missing from her quarters when I finally allowed the summoning spell to snare me in its trap in order to bring me to her in this strange human realm. For a moment, I thought there must be a mistake.

There isn't. There can't be. Just breathing in her lingering scent... the way my body reacted to it, my cock hardening for the first time in so godsdamn long... I already knew she was meant to be mine before I even saw her.

Then I did, and she has my heart in her dainty, wee hands from the first moment I ever set eyes on her.

I was careful. Remembering Susanna's stories and

her warnings, I immediately traded my solid demon form for my shadows. I am still a formidable hunter, even in this shape, but I can make myself just small enough to fit in the containment circle she's prepared for my arrival.

I don't know what kind of magic my female has, only that I would burn too much essence if I tried to escape it without her permission. She must have set it out so that she could be sure she summoned the right demon; assuming she does not know that the spell she used to call me to her is the matefinder spell that already marks her as mine.

So I waited. Hovering in place, trembling in anticipation, I waited for her to return to me, and I was rewarded with a vision of her beauty when she entered her quarters again, clutching a towel and some sort of blue drink in an odd vessel.

In so many ways, she reminds me of Susanna, only infinitely more lovely because Susanna loves Duke Haures, and this female will desire me for her male. Her skin is that colorless human shade, like a faint, sickly pink to my strapped red, with dim eyes that still seem to shine like the honey a demon can only find in the capital city where the buzz-bugs live amongst Susanna's oasis garden.

Her hair is darker than honey, longer than even mine, and twisted like a thick piece of twine. She has it settled over her delicate shoulder, curving around a breast that is far more bountiful than any Soleil demoness.

She is wee even so. Barely higher than a demon spawn, if she came close enough to me, her crown might reach my chest—and that's if I lower myself to her. I do not mind, though. She is dainty, and I am strong. I will protect her from any danger that might come for her, and I wordlessly add that vow to the mate's promise that's singing in my lonely heart as our eyes meet.

"Dagon," I tell her, speaking in Sombran because that's the only language I can speak in. Thanks to Susanna, I've learned enough of the human language to know that, in human, 'uxor' translates to 'mate'. I might not be able to tell her more than that until the essence exchange, but at least I can say, "Dagon mate."

I had hoped she would understand—but that's when she dropped her belongings and began to scream.

I don't know how to react to that. I'm not often screamed at, and through the fated tie that exists between my mate and me, I sense her fright. It wounds me, and I crouch low, my eyes glowing brightly to show her that it is I, her male, and she has no reason to be afraid.

It does not work—and realizing that my human

mate is as skittish as a prey beast in the shadows, I change my tactic.

I observe her. Hiding my claws and my fangs in my shadows while dimming my gaze… I let her get used to me.

She seems more sure of herself when she glances at the protective circle, remembering that I cannot approach her so long as I am in it. I'd much prefer to go to my mate, to touch her, to hold her, to show her that she's mine, but if she needs me to stay here while she accepts all of that, I shall.

Besides, all it will take is a simple touch. From my experience—what Susanna told me, and what I've learned from the other Sombra demons fortunate enough to have a human for a female—humans don't guard their essence the way that my people do. Susanna gave hers away to Duke Haures immediately. Once her kin was mature, so did Amelia to Nox.

Then there was the artist from Nuit. Malphas. Nox was a hunter, just like I am, though he came from a different village than mine; he was also from Nuit while I hail from Caol. Malphas is another demon who found his mate in a human woman. The white-haired female is currently expecting his spawn, the two of them also living in this human world.

Nox has done the same. Only a cycle ago, Sammael chose to forsake his role as Duke Haures's head mage to join his own human mate in this realm.

That won't be me.

Whatever it takes, I will find a way to claim my mate, and once I have, she will follow me to Sombra. My debt to Susanna repaid, I will return to Caol, hunting and providing for my beautiful female for the rest of our existence together.

Now, if only I knew the name of the female who will one day brand my chest...

I cannot ask her, not until I know her language; though, as soon as I do, I'll have her essence and know everything about her, including how best to woo her. For now, I must wait for her to understand that I am the male she called forth with the matefinder spell.

And I am, even if I'm not the most patient of males.

During a hunt, I must be. I've trained myself to be. Bonding my female to me forever... I had hoped I wouldn't have to be patient, but I will do anything for my one true mate.

So I wait. I wait. I wait some more, and I watch as she finally tears her dull honey gaze away from me before slipping toward the massive nest in the center of her quarters.

Ah. I think I understand. Nestled on the edge, I see the *Grimoire du Sombra*, the book that hosts the matefinder spell that first brought Susanna to Sombra.

I've held it in my own claws before. Without Duke Haures knowing, I've even glanced at the matefinder spell. I never read it—this is human magic, and I am demon—but it has two parts to it: the summoning spell that snares a true mate, and the mate's promise that begins the process that ties us to each other for the rest of our immortal existence.

She must have read the first half otherwise I would not be itching to prowl around the tight containment circle as I am. Maybe now that she has accepted I am her mate, she will use the text as a guide to recite the mate's promise to me.

I hold my breath as she props open the book, flipping the pages to one in particular.

Her pale face creases as she murmurs something I do not understand. It's not the mate's promise, though, and before she can begin the fateful vow, she slams the book closed again, tossing it back onto the bedding.

I swallow my growl. I would only frighten her again if I did, and that won't do.

But if she won't come to me, *touch me* to give me her essence so that I will be able to understand her human tongue, then I must find a way to give her mine. She'll know Sombra instinctively, and though I'm risking the mate sickness increasing my already potent need for her, it will be worth the struggle to at least communicate with my mate.

The sensation of fire starts even before I push against the invisible barrier keeping me inside of her magic circle. My claws are impervious to the flames, but beneath my shadowy fingers, I start to burn.

I don't care. I feed the magic a little of my essence, hoping it'll be enough to reach out to my mate.

As soon as I break free of the circle, four fingertips crossing past that boundary, my shadowy flesh is instantly engulfed. Gritting my teeth, my fangs biting into my skin, I push harder until my forearm is freed—and also in flames.

I've never known such agony. The closest was when the arkoda slashed my chest open with its powerful claws, when I was too wounded to battle the beast or heal my grievous injuries before it slaughtered me; if Susanna hadn't been there to save my existence, it would have. Knowing that this pain is crucial to attracting my human mate, I endure it, begging the gods that it will be enough to draw her closer.

Closer.

Closer...

"Uxor mi," I spit out through my clenched jaw. I continue in Sombran as I plead, "My mate, *please*."

Does she understand me after all? I'm not sure, but when her honey eyes reflect the fire as my essence burns for her... I no longer see fear.

At least, she is not afraid *of* me. Afraid for me, perhaps—and that's when she screams again, and it only matters that I have frightened my mate once more.

What a waste of my essence. Rather than draw her near me, my mate darts across her quarters and...

Through the flickering flames, I see her grab something between her hands. Rushing toward me again, she twists it, opening it. I don't know what it is, but when she tosses its contents at the circle and I'm splashed with it, it's obvious that it is water.

Some of the water dampens the flames. It's not enough to erase the magic in the containment circle or completely put out the fire, but I'm so stunned by my mate's quick thinking and desire to protect me—her hunter, her *male*—that I draw my hand back.

The last of the fire goes out.

She's holding her vessel with one hand. With the other, she reaches for me, taking hold of my arm.

Her chilly fingers find my flesh beneath my shadows. The sensation is so pleasurable, it's all I can do not to jerk my lower form and release my seed at her feet.

That would not make the best impression on my female, I'm sure. So I grit my teeth and allow her to explore me, even as she rattles in her human language.

"Ryu ok? Uwer on fyr. Duzthis hurt?" She pokes my flesh. "Howsdat?"

I'm not sure what she is saying, but I sense her worry for me and am touched by her reaction.

She... she saved me.

Like Susanna did with the arkoda, my soft-hearted mate braved her fear to quench the flames burning through my essence. And not only did she do that, but she reached through the containment circle, grabbing my hand as though to make sure the fire didn't damage my shadows.

She *touched* me—and though it might be considered ruthless by some demons, I am determined to make this female mine.

And that begins with giving her my essence.

A jolt passes between us, turning her worry to sudden confusion—and surprise.

Of course. My essence has just reached my human mate, and I give her every last drop that I didn't burn with my reckless need to get close to her. I thought it a waste before. I was wrong. It was worth the pain because giving myself to her... there is no greater pleasure.

At least until I finally give her my cock and bond my one true mate to me forever, that is...

Clank.

She drops her water vessel. It hits the hard floor beneath her before rolling away.

My mate doesn't notice. Oh, no. She is staring wide-eyed at her male.

I smile. With my essence settling into her wee human body, she will instinctively know that I am no danger to her. That, when I smile, my fangs are nothing to fear, just like she has no reason to be afraid of her demon.

I bow my head in respect to her, letting my shadowy hair fall forward, covering my bare chest.

Bare for now—but not for much longer...

"Ah. I thank you, my mate." With my gaze dipped, I don't see her reaction. I do, however, hear her gasp of surprise as she instantly translates Sombran into her human tongue. "I am Dagon. Your humble hunter, and forever your mate."

CHAPTER 6

DRAGON WITHOUT THE R

SIERRA

What the fuck just happened?

One second, I was trying to figure out what my next step was going to be since the weird book doesn't seem to be much help. The next? I don't know exactly what went wrong, but the shadow creature *thing* was on fire!

It wasn't all of him. Just the part of his arm that he managed to stick out of the circle trapping him. From fingertips to elbow, he was all flames and, not gonna lie, I panicked for a second.

Luckily for both of us, that panic only lasts for a second before my ass kicks into gear. Next to my bed, I have a nightstand where I usually keep my white noise machine, a pair of headphones, whatever book or magazine I'm reading at any given moment, and an oversized steel water bottle so that I can keep hydrated overnight.

Billie's always on my case, making sure I drink enough water. I try, but more often than not, my tumbler is still at least halfway full come morning. For once, that works to my benefit since I grab it, twisting off the lid, tossing that and the plastic straw to the floor before splashing the monster's arm with all the water left inside.

The fire goes out immediately. At the same time, the monster pulls his arm back into the circle.

You know what the problem with this strange creature looking like he's something the darkest shadows I've ever seen spat out?

Up close, I can kind of make out the shape of a nose, a chin, individual arms and fingers within the shifting, inky blackness. However, since his entire form looks like something I might make if I attempted to actually cook for myself, that means it's impossible for me to tell how badly the fire hurt him.

I care, too. Because I read the spell that brought him here? Because it was the chalk and the salt that I set up that's keeping him trapped within the circle? Probably. It doesn't matter. Deep down, I've always been a soft touch. Whether it's a cat or a monster, I can't stand to see anyone suffer.

I have to check. I have to know. And maybe it's not

the smartest thing to do, grabbing onto the injured arm of a huge-ass monster who already showed me his *fangs*, but before I can think better of what I'm about to do, I reach for him.

"Are you okay? You were on fire! Does this hurt?" I grab him. "How's that?"

It only hits me as I make contact that he's a *shadow* creature. How exactly do I expect to check him out? Shouldn't my hand go right through his form?

You'd think—and you'd be wrong.

My fingers do pass through the first inch of him. The tips and my nails dip through the outer edge of his shadows, but then I find firm flesh. It's hot, so hot it reminds me of hopping into a scalding shower before checking the temp, but not so bad that my skin sizzles against his. Like, it's *hot*, but not burning, and I try to touch him lightly so I don't hurt him.

The big monster rumbles the instant I make contact. It doesn't sound like a warning type of noise, though. Neither does he sound like he's in pain.

Honestly? It's more the opposite of that.

I doubt he understands what I'm saying. I prattle away in English regardless, but all he does is stay still and preen a bit as I hold onto him. And then, before I can remember myself and that *he's a shadow monster in my bedroom*, something even weirder happens.

It's a jolt. A shock. Something sparks, passing

between us, and I stumble backward suddenly when it feels like someone has pushed me in the chest.

My cup falls, and I stare up at him.

It wasn't the monster. It couldn't be. I was so close, watching him the whole time, and I was even still gripping his arm when that sensation barreled into me. And yet... my sudden instinct warns that, whatever happened now, he's definitely responsible for it.

His vivid red gaze follows me as I break our connection.

Then, to my utter surprise, he shows me his fangs again.

I whimper. Can't help it. I whimper, and he lowers his head. A massive sheet of dark, dark hair falls forward, shielding his red eyes. His horns are pointed at me, and that has me taking another step away from him even as he speaks again.

"Ah. I thank you, my mate."

What the fuck?

My whimper turns into a shocked gasp.

Because that? That's not English. It's *not*. Everything from the cadence to the accent, plus the harsh syllables that surprisingly sound melodic in his deep voice... it all reminds me of those strange words that I read out of the spellbook.

He spoke to me just now in another language—but as if a translator app was downloaded straight into my brain, I *understood* him.

Just like I do when he goes on to add, "I am Dagon. Your humble hunter, and forever your mate."

"My *what*?"

Holy shit. When I screeched... the same fucking thing happened. I *thought* in English, I *know* what I was trying to say, but the words that came out of my mouth?

Not English. It's not any language I know, either.

But he does.

The big monster lifts his head so that I can peek right into those glowing eyes of his again. "My mate. The one female meant as my own, and who I've waited five long centuries for."

Five... centuries?

Five *centuries*?

I open my mouth. Nothing comes out. Not in English, or that monster language I'm suddenly fluent in.

Five hundred years...

What?

Okay. Take a second, Sierra. That makes sense, right? He's a monster. Maybe he's immortal. Maybe he's long-lived. Maybe, when he says five centuries, that's demon-speak for fifty—

Remember that sensation I was shoved from, like, two minutes ago? Out of nowhere, it seems to travel, only instead of being pushed, my head feels super full and very heavy all of a sudden.

And I know... just like I know that I'm speaking another language... that he *is* five hundred years old *and* immortal, and that he one hundred percent believes that his gods have rewarded his wait with *me*.

That already he adores me, and while he is a hunter who eats meat, when he gazes down at me, gobbling me up isn't what he wants to do to me—at least, not in the bad way.

I'm not his dinner.

I'm his *wife*.

WHAT THE FUCK IS GOING ON?

That's all I can think as I put some distance between the monster and me. I take a deep breath, then another. I don't stop until that stuffy feeling in my head fades enough that I'm the only one rattling around in there. Once I do, I pull a smile to my face, directing it at the shadowy creature.

Honestly? Only fifteen years of media training is keeping me from completely losing my shit right now.

I get a pass for losing it when I first found him in my bedroom. No matter what, I think even the most blasé of people might be taken aback to walk into their personal space and be confronted by the size, the horns, the claws, and the glowing eyes peering at them.

Now, I've seen some shit. More than most people

have in their entire lifetimes, and I've only just hit thirty-one. That means it takes a lot to surprise me, and even more to shock me.

A shadow monster—no, something corrects inside of me, a shadow *demon...* a shadow demon who thinks he's destined to be my demon husband definitely tops the list.

And while I'm secretly shaking in my metaphorical boots right now, you wouldn't know it to look at me.

"Okay. Hi. I just want to make sure I understand this." Is that even possible? I hope so. "I... what? Read that spell and you're the one who answered?"

"Aye. I'm the only one who could."

Right. Because this giant monster is supposed to be my true love. That's what the spell said I was manifesting, and there's no denying I manifested something.

I manifested Dagon.

As though the demon can tell exactly what I'm thinking—and who knows, maybe he *can*—he tells me, "I am your one true mate. And you are mine."

Sorry, big guy. That won't be happening.

Still, no denying that, the more I look at him, the more he's got me curious. He's obviously trapped behind the salt. Just sticking his hand out of it burned him, and whatever he did to me, something tells me that was one of the most painful things he's ever done —and he did it to get closer to me.

Though there's no reason for me to be, I'm pretty

sure he's not about to test the protective circle again. He's stuck in there. I also have the sudden understanding that he'd rather relive that pain tenfold than ever hurt his mate.

Hurt *me*.

I'm safe. And maybe I'm being reckless, trusting that when I know better than most how quickly a contained situation can become dangerous, but I'm still incredibly intrigued.

And talking to a sentient monster seems a whole lot more interesting than going through weeks-old fan mail right about now.

Even if I shouldn't be able to talk to him at all.

I rub my throat, grateful that my earlier scream didn't do any further damage or create another polyp. Just in case, though, I speak softer than before. "Is that why I can talk to you? That we can understand each other?"

"That's from my essence," he says gruffly, drifting closer to the edge of the circle—and closer to me. "Everything I am... it's yours now. My heart. My life. My devotion." Forming a fist, tucking those mega claws out of sight, he taps his shadowy chest. "*I am* yours."

Okay. Maybe I'm a little too dirty-minded sometimes, but when he says 'essence' like that, I can't stop myself from thinking he's talking about semen. A moment later, I know the true reason, and I'm not sure what it says about me that I'm a little disappointed it isn't.

His essence is like his soul. All of his thoughts, his memories, his life experience... even his demon language... was passed from him to me when I grabbed his arm.

It's a demon thing, I guess. Still, there's a pretty obvious reason why I got 'essence' and come mixed up. Though I shouldn't know instinctively what he means when he calls me his 'mate', it's exactly that: this monster expects to fuck me, claim me, and make me his.

That's why he told me that he's mine—because he has this insane idea that I belong to him.

Get in line, buddy. There's thousands of guys like you who all think they own Whiskey Rose.

"Yeah, no... I'm sorry. What did you say your name is again?"

"I am Dagon—"

Dagon. "Like Dragon without the 'r'. Cool. Got it. Anyway—"

It's his turn to interrupt me. I guess it's only fair since I did cut him off before.

"—protector of the Duchess of Sombra, proud Sombra demon male, fierce hunter, and fated mate to a legendary human."

I guess I'm supposed to be impressed.

I shrug. "Yeah? Well, I'm Whiskey Rose."

His expression is blank.

Weird. He's the one who called me legendary, so I just assumed he knew who I was. From what I gather from that download, an essence exchange between demons—Sombra demons... oh, like the *Grimoire du Sombra*—and their mates works both ways. I get his, he gets mine, and we get a happily-ever-after.

Phew. Maybe it's a good thing that he doesn't have mine because, yeah... no way in hell am I a monster's mate.

I am, however, just as proud of my accomplishments as he is, and probably even more vain.

"Pop star? Winner of a Best New Artist Grammy? Actress? No? What about Maxim's Sexiest Woman Alive, two years running?" True, that was when I was nineteen and twenty, but it counts—especially after the way I was perved on even more by guys three times my age after my covers came out. "Not ringing a bell, demon?"

His brow furrows, fine lines bracketing the ridges over his long nose. "I hear no bell, my mate, and I don't know who Maxim is, but you are not his one true mate, whether he considered you a female he wanted to mate with or not. That honor will be mine."

Like I said, it wasn't really an honor... hang on—

"Maxim's not a person. It's a..." I pause. I want to say 'magazine', but I draw a blank. It's almost like there's no equivalent in the monster's language. Huh. Turning around, I grab the book I left on the end of my bed. I hold it up, tapping the cover with my palm. "It's like a book, only with pictures."

"There are pictures of my mate for other males to see?"

Wow. Poor unsuspecting demon. He has no idea.

I place the book down again. "You could say that."

He's quiet for a moment. "They should be lucky. You are a very beautiful female. As long as you don't mate other males, I will share your pictures with them."

It's so nice to have his permission—

Wait. Again with the mating—and it's even more obvious this time that he means fucking. Only...

God help me, but I'm a perv. A horny perv at that. Because as I look him over again, keeping quiet, all I can think about is how exactly a monster of his size can mate a human like me... and if he even has the equipment to do so.

I'm getting used to him. Before, I could pick out his chin, his nose, his fingers. Now? Peering closer, looking through his shadows, I'm pretty damn sure that's one hell of a shadow dick sticking out from his nondescript groin.

He takes in a breath, almost like he's smelling something. "*Whiskey Rose...*"

Oh, no. That was my fuck-up. I'm so used to introducing myself as my alter ego, readying myself for their shock and awe at meeting a celebrity, I did the same to this demon. But the way he growled my stage name just now?

My sudden lust has my raspy voice going just a little throaty. "Sierra. When I'm home, I'm Sierra."

Dagon doesn't miss a beat. "*Sierra...*"

I shiver. What the hell?

I dart out my tongue, licking my bottom lip quickly as I lift my gaze up—and then up some more.

Jesus Christ, he's tall.

Distraction. I'm always looking for a distraction, and right now I need one from how curious I am about a demon's dick.

"How tall are you?"

I gotta ask. My apartment has high-vaulted ceilings since it's such an old, classic building, and while his horns aren't scratching them, he's still towering over me even from this distance.

I've always been attracted to a tall guy. I guess when it comes to shadow monsters, that interest is enough to cross species.

And, yeah... I don't know what the hell that says about me, either, but it's still probably not anything to be proud of.

Eh. I'm used to it.

The demon, on the other hand, might not be just quite.

Dagon blinks. His glowing eyes wink out, his whole

form going dark for a split second before they're back on. "How... tall?"

I gesture at him. "Yeah. I mean. You're pretty fucking huge—"

His chest puffs out. "That's in my shadows. Let me show you my demon."

<hr>

OH, MAMA. I'M IN TROUBLE.

Up until this moment, I knew he was a demon. A *shadow* demon. This little voice inside of me that I'm working hard to ignore reiterates that he's a *Sombra* demon, as if that makes any difference.

It doesn't. At least, not to me.

But back to my point. Dagon is a shadow demon, and his pitch-black skin and slightly amorphous shape sells that. In a way, he reminds me of the bogeyman I used to dream about when I was a kid. A dark creature with glowing red eyes that haunted me when I slept, though when impish Sierra mentioned that to her mother, she got tossed melatonin first, then Benadryl to try to get rid of my 'nightmare'.

It didn't work. All that happened was that she drugged me to put me to sleep so she didn't have to deal with me outside of lessons and auditions.

They weren't nightmares, either. Honestly? My mom tried to make me a star starting when I was *four*.

Playing with the bogeyman in my dreams was the only break I got from my true nightmare: my mom, who always wanted to live vicariously through me.

I wonder if that's why, subconsciously, I wasn't *as* afraid to see Dagon as I might've been. Don't get me wrong. I was close to shitting myself for a second there; puke wasn't the only thing I struggled to keep back. But I calmed down a little once I got a better look at him—until he bared his fangs at me, of course—and now that his essence tells me that was his attempt at a *smile* and that he would never, ever hurt his true mate... I'm suddenly a lot more interested in learning about this five-hundred-year-old demon than being afraid he's going to attack me.

I just hope the essence he passed over to me can be trusted. It almost makes me wish humans could do something similar. Do you know how much easier life would be if you shook hands with someone and, in an instant, knew their thoughts, memories, *and* motives?

I never would've gotten involved with Jared in the first place, I'll tell you that much...

But while I'm experiencing some of what Dagon is, thanks to whatever he did to me, I don't know *every-thing* right off the bat. I guess it's going to trickle down, maybe, or only pop into my brain when necessary.

And discovering that Dagon isn't only made up of shadows... that's probably so ingrained into who he is, the essence forgot to fill me in on that little tidbit until he shifts shapes right in front of me.

CHAPTER 7
HOW TALL?

SIERRA

Did I think he was huge before? That's nothing compared to now as I get my first real look at Dagon as a demon.

I'd put him at no less than seven feet, and that's not even counting his horns. And while his long, thick hair, pointed claws, and his sharp horns are still as black as his shadows, his demon skin is a dark, rusted red color that makes his bright red eyes shine even brighter in comparison.

Dagon told me he was a hunter in his demon world, but if he'd said he was a bodybuilder or a wrestler—if this Sombra place even has those—I wouldn't have questioned that at all. He has muscles upon muscles, and nothing covering his chest. No hair there, either, and I see a pair of dark brown nipples popping out of his sculpted pecs.

His ears are pointed; add that to the red skin and he has a decidedly swarthy, almost devilish appearance. Apart from the ridges over his long nose, the rest of his features are surprisingly human-like. His jaw is chiseled, his cheekbones sharp, and he has surprisingly soft lips that I should not be staring at right now.

So, instead, being Sierra... I drop my gaze to his bottom half.

I shouldn't be disappointed that, from his waist down, he's covered in more shadows. They almost look like leather pants, giving me a clue about how thick his thighs are, but though his chest is bare, the rest of him isn't.

Considering all of his talk about 'mates', I should be grateful he's not already flashing me.

Should be...

I shake my head, trying to get back on topic.

Wait—

What topic?

Oh, yeah. That's right. I'd asked him how tall he was, and in response, he showed me what he really looks like. And maybe this is the last thing I should be worried about right now, but I gotta know.

It's like when I used to run into fans out on the

street. Inevitably, they would either ask me who I wrote a certain song about, or bluntly mention Jared. It didn't matter that our scandalous break-up happened a decade ago. In the public eye, we never should've broken up at all. America's couple and all that fucking bullshit. They didn't care that Jared broke my heart when he cheated with Tandy. We looked good on the red carpet together, and that's all that mattered.

And, no, I'm not still bitter at all…

Anyway. While Whiskey Rose has to deal with that, I imagine that most guys topping six and half feet or so constantly get asked about their height. Tilting my head back, looking up at Dagon, I know better than to ask—and I do it anyway.

"Can I measure you?"

It's a fair enough question. He obviously doesn't know the same kind of measurement units we use here in the States so it's not like he can tell me how tall he is in a way I'll understand, but he can let me see for myself.

"Will it please you, my mate?"

That's a strange way of putting it.

"I get curious sometimes," I admit. "If you're worried it'll hurt, it won't." I go and grab my phone, shaking it at him, showing it off. Forget about calling for help… I think I can handle this myself. "Look. I got an app."

He bows his head. "Prepare your app. You may do to me whatever you like, Sierra."

Oh, Dagon saying my name like that should not be half as sexy as it is.

I snort. Remembering how badly I wanted to get laid earlier, I tell him, "You might regret saying that, demon."

"Never."

Hm. We'll see. "Straighten up. I want to get your full height."

He does. "Like this?"

"Eighty-six inches, holy shit." I quickly do the math in my head. "You're seven-four! Wait. I want to get the horns now."

Again, he poses while I trigger the point at his feet, moving my phone until it hits the tip of his left horn.

"Seven more inches! That means you're almost eight feet with your horns!"

Later, I'll admit that my excitement might've given him the wrong—or maybe *right*—idea. I went from screaming at him, keeping my distance, to grabbing him, then acting amazed over his size.

Dagon is quiet for a moment. He's obviously thinking about something, and after a few seconds, he says gruffly, "Do you like your males large? Does that please you?"

Again with the 'please you'... I shrug, slipping my

phone into my pocket. I won't need it yet, but just in case, I'm gonna keep it in reach.

"I guess so," I say at last.

My gaze drops again. If the rest of him is proportionate to his height, I can only imagine what those shadows are covering up.

A moment later, I don't *have* to imagine.

When Dagon was talking about size, I couldn't help but think about other parts of him. Looks like the demon has the same idea.

As though they were never there, the shadows covering his lower half simply vanish.

"See, my mate? I am also large in other places. But don't you worry. I know of other demons who were given human mates. I am large, but we will fit well."

He means what he says. Not sure I believe him, though.

How can I when I get my first real look at what he kept hidden beneath those shadows?

Huge is an understatement. And, yeah, I was right about him being in proportion. On Dagon, his erection seems to fit his oversized body. But when I compare it to me?

As tempting as it is to open up my measuring app again, I just manage to restrain myself. He's gotta be at least ten inches, if not more, but it's the girth that has my eyes bugging out of my head.

There's just no way that we will fit, but that doesn't

stop me from suddenly thinking about what it would be like if we tried…

"Sierra. Let me out of the circle," he growls in demand. "Now."

I glance up at him. I'm not scared… not this time… but his growl is enough to rip me out of my fantasy. "What?"

"You must. Only you can use your magic to break the containment circle. Release me. You need me. Let me tend to my female."

Magic? I don't have any magic. I mean, I guess I could use my foot to erase the chalk and create an opening in the salt to let him out. I figure that would work, but—

"What do you mean, tend to"—I can't say 'your female' like that 'cause that just sounds icky—"*me*?"

In his demon shape, when Dagon breathes in deeply, I see his nostrils flutter. "You already grow ready for your male. I will help you prepare to take me."

Yes—I mean no!

Fuck a monster? Am I serious?

Because when he says 'take', when he repeatedly refers to me as his 'mate', there's no doubt in my mind what he really means. Showing off his cock like that was just the icing on the cake there.

It's one thing to have a moment of weakness to

fantasize about fucking a shadow demon. It's something completely different to actually do it.

I leave him in the circle, taking a few steps away in the hope that he can't realize just how badly I kind of want to say 'let's go for it'.

"This is crazy." Am *I* crazy? Did my public meltdown lead me to imagining I could do magic and summon my very own demon love slave? "How is this possible? I didn't even know demons were *real*."

Dagon huffs. I'll give the big demon credit, though. When he understands that I'm not about to let him out, then fall back on the bed with my legs spread all because he growled at me, he doesn't push. He doesn't insist.

Instead, he responds to my comment.

"Of course not. No one in the human world is allowed to unless they are a mate. It's Duke Haures's first law."

My brain pulses, the beginning of a headache that I really don't want to deal with right now. Worse, when he says 'Duke Haures', I actually get a good idea who he is without Dagon having to explain.

"The ruler of your world."

His eyes flash. "Yes. My essence told you."

I don't admit a damn thing. Instead, refusing to rely on his essence again, I ask, "What's the first law?"

"In Sombra, the duke has many. But the first law was

established two millennia ago when he took the throne." Throne? And he's a duke, not a king? Weird. "He insists that only other demon realms can have contact. Unless a human summons a demon to this world, we're forbidden to visit. The punishment is severe for breaking that law."

I don't even want to guess what an immortal shadow demon thinks is a severe punishment.

"But I know about you now," I point out.

"Yes. And you are my mate, so the first law has not been broken."

Okay. I admit, I walked right into that one myself.

"So you're here. But Sombra is where you live, not Earth. Not New York. So... how do we get you back there?"

Dagon shakes his head. "We cannot."

There has to be a way. If there's a law in place, that means it's *possible* for demons to travel between worlds. It's just not allowed. Assuming human time and demon time are about the same, two millennia ago is, like, ancient times. Is that why we have legends of demons? They used to walk among us before this ruler decided that wasn't allowed?

Makes sense to me.

Let's say I did summon Dagon. All evidence points to that being the case. However, that just means he can accept that I'm not interested in being a monster's bride. He goes back, I clean up this mess, and no one ever has to know what happened.

Good?

Good.

"I cannot return to Sombra. Not without you. You summoned me with the matefinder spell. I am your mate. We have the beginning of a bond. Once you give yourself to me completely, we will be together forever."

Not good.

"Well, I can't leave New York."

I can't even leave my apartment these days.

"There is time. Let me get to know you, Sierra. Use my essence to learn your male. Let me prove you will have no mate better than I."

I rub my temple. Fuck. My head feels so stuffed, and that headache is getting worse and worse every time he mentions something that triggers another question that pops into my head. He didn't mention it himself, but when he said that we have time, all I can think about is a huge glowing moon next to a darker, larger in a shadow-filled sky.

What the—

"What's up with the gold moon?"

The question was triggered, but before Dagon can answer me, I already know what he's going to say. "It's a... deadline? For me to accept you, and you to finalize your bond with me?"

"Aye. I must claim you as my bonded mate before then or one of Duke Haures's soldiers will drag me back to Sombra."

I get a flash of... chains. Golden ones, shining even brighter than the strange second moon that also popped into my brain.

No. *No*. This *is* crazy, and I've got to stop digging into the essence of Dagon. It's too tempting, simply knowing everything about this demon at just a whim.

It's not fair, either.

The truth is that, gold moon or not, he's wasting his time with me.

He won't be here forever. He *can't* be. There's no way in hell I can be a demon's mate. No matter how desperate he is to claim me as his, I can't let that happen. But just because bonding my soul to his before this deadline is a no go, that doesn't mean I can't take this opportunity to actually get to know him for real.

Why not enjoy his company while I can?

I've seen a lot during my career. I've experienced so much, too. Gotta say, though, that discovering seven-foot-tall demons with horns, massive cocks, and an ability to smell when I'm lusting over said cock because I'm one horny bitch who kind of wants to give him a whirl... that's definitely a new one for me.

But that doesn't mean I'm going to be his mate.

I can't, and the more Dagon gets to know me, he'll understand that.

He's stuck here, though. Until this deadline of his

passes, and since I have no idea when exactly that could be, I give him one of my own.

"Fine. You can stay with me for the weekend." I frown. The weird demon word that comes out when I try to say 'weekend' doesn't seem like a close translation to me. Maybe they don't have the concept of what a week or a weekend is in his language. Whatever. "It'll just be me and Three until then, and your law says humans can't see you. He's not a human." Though try telling him that when he wants a piece of whatever I'm eating. "But if you try anything funny, I've got more chalk and salt. I'll put you right back in that circle if I have to."

And, hopefully, the gold moon will pass, and he'll go back to that Sombra place long before Billie returns to the apartment and I'll have to deal with any of this.

Or regret what I've already agreed to.

<hr>

WHAT DO YOU DO WITH A NEARLY EIGHT-FOOT-TALL demon who constantly looks at you like he's starving and you're his favorite meal?

If you're me, you feed him.

I needed to eat. Once I got over my shock that my true love is a *demon*, my stomach reminded me that I was hungry with a quite embarrassing rumble.

Instead of seeming confused that humans can

make such a sound, Dagon nodded his head knowingly. "You need food. Are there hunting grounds nearby where I can provide my mate with a meal?"

I didn't even know how to answer that. I guess, when he told me he was a hunter, it never clicked that, in his demon world, he hunts for his food.

Well, he can't do that here. I reminded him about the first law, and explained that we're currently in New York City. The closest patch of greenery to me is Central Park, and it's so crowded around the clock, he's risking being seen.

The demon tried to tell me that he could hide in order to provide for his mate, but I cut him off quickly by showing him all of the choices available on my food delivery app.

Poor demon. He's so eager to please me, he listened to the different options though there's no way he knows what any of them are. In the end, he told me he would be grateful to eat anything his mate provided *him,* and by that point, I'd given up telling him that I'm not his mate.

He's convinced, and I'm stuck with a lovesick demon who rumbles when he speaks, and whose low growl already has me creaming my panties.

Food might help. At the very least, it's the best distraction I could come up with.

It's twenty after seven when my phone buzzes. When it does, I jump, thinking it's a message from

Billie, letting me know she's on her way back at last. It isn't. It's from Dave at the desk, letting me know he's sending Sal up with my order.

Since I felt bad and let Dagon out of the containment circle, he's hovered around my room, marveling at all of the decorations I have. I let him because that means he isn't staring intently at me anymore, though I can't stop myself from watching him.

Not out of fear, though. This is pure curiosity that only gets egged on when I refuse to use his essence to satisfy all of my questions.

The odd thing is that, essence or not, I *should* be afraid. For one thing, he's a *demon*. An immortal demon, according to the info that keeps popping into my brain without me searching for it. He *is* a hunter, and when some shaggy, blackish bear-ish creature flashes before my eyes, it's easy to see why he's so proud of that fact.

If I had to face off against a *nine-foot-tall* horned bear and survived, I'd be proud, too.

But this download of Dagon gets weirder and weirder. As soon as I have that fleeting thought about the beast he was hunting, another face appears. A human woman, this time, and one who definitely isn't *me*. I mean, she's paler for one. Younger for another. My hair is tawny, hers is a rich brown. There's no way to confuse us, but *I*'ve never seen her before.

With this demon duke's first law in place, how did Dagon?

I don't ask. It feels too intrusive, questioning this stranger about things I see in my head. And, true, he gave me permission when he passed his essence over to me, but still. It doesn't feel *right* to ask, especially when I won't know him for long.

But because I know about the law now, I'm careful not to break it. That's why, when Sal's coming up the elevator, I point at Dagon.

"I'm going to get our food. You stay here."

"My mate—"

I narrow my eyes at him in a slight warning. Okay. Maybe I have one more refusal in me.

Dagon clears his throat. "Sierra. You must allow me to follow you."

And let the Dorado delivery guy see him?

"No. And if you ask again, I'm grabbing the chalk. Okay?"

"I— yes." He pauses, then says, "Will you go far?"

Does he think I'm going to take the chance to escape and leave him alone in my apartment?

"Nah. Just past the gallery." I shrug. "I can't leave the apartment, remember?"

He nods, though I don't think he really understands.

That's okay. He doesn't have to.

I'm just tipping Sal when, suddenly, the smoke alarm goes off.

My head whips around, my wig fanning behind me as I search for the source of the high-pitched screech. I have no idea why I'm hearing it. Sure, Dagon was burning earlier, but I let him out of the circle so the fire is a thing of the past. There's no reason why the smoke alarm should be going off...

Right?

Shit.

Sal looks around, too. "What's that?"

Good question. "I just remembered... oh, jeez. I think I left a pot of water on to boil for some tea." I tap my throat, reminding him why I'm back at the Dorado, then shoo him toward the door. "Thank you for the food. And don't worry about that. I'll go turn the burner off and fan the kitchen. I'll be fine. Okay, thanks, bye!"

Does he buy it? Probably not. But despite the wig and glasses I threw on to answer the door, Sal's worked here almost as long as I've had the penthouse. He knows who I am, he appreciates the fifty I just slipped him, and has always been the epitome of discreet.

Unless the building starts burning down, he'll accept the excuse I gave him and go back to the front desk without another word—and that's exactly what he does.

Once the elevator doors close, I drop the bags of food to the floor, rip off my wig, tossing it as I take off for the kitchen.

In case Billie and I ever do decide to cook, Roy insisted on a fire extinguisher hanging within reach. I snag it now, then head for the bedroom, hoping the entire way that Dagon hasn't done something to burn down my apartment after all.

CHAPTER 8
AN UNGEZ

DAGON

Sierra has my essence. We have a fledgling bond stretching between us. Because it is so new, and it isn't finalized, there are other rules that we must follow apart from just Duke Haures's first law.

The most important one?

I am a Sombra demon. I was born of the shadows, and immortal as I am, when I eventually tire of this existence, I always accepted that the shadows would have to take me first. My set of bones will be one of thousands that litter the ash fields on the edge of Sombra.

That was before. For five hundred years, I believed that, but now I have found my mate.

I will never tire of this existence.

From the moment she gives me her essence, the mate's promise, and her cunt, our bond will be unbreakable. She will also be immortal, and with Sierra at my side, we will have forever.

Don't we already? Our life together has only just begun, and I've never been more content that I am in this odd human realm.

I do have one regret. If only I had warned her of the Sombran decree—cast down from our gods, and woven into our shadows—that insists unbonded mates stay near each other until we do as the gods expect of us and finalize our fated tie.

Legend says that Sombra demons are shadows in more than just our shapes. If our mate walks away—bonded or not—we will always follow. However, because Sierra and I are *not* bonded yet, I need to be near her more than I need to breathe.

But she refused me before, and I discovered that my desire to do as my mate says is even greater than my demonic instincts.

She told me to stay. I stayed. Even as the fire consumed my shadows again, burning me up because she went too far... I refused to leave her quarters.

It doesn't hurt; at least, not much. If I still had my essence, it would've been agony... but if I had my essence, I would not suffer to see Sierra leave me.

I'd rather burn than know we have nothing tying

us together, even if I regret frightening my skittish mate once more.

I was still engulfed in flames when she threw the door open, dashing into her personal quarters, carrying a large red vial in her hands. Again, she screeches, but just scenting her, taking the smell of her into my lungs... it's enough to fight the flames.

That's what the large red vial is for, I learn, and why I heard something howling even louder than Sierra herself when I frightened her. My mate's lair is prone to burning, with layers of protection against it, including a high-pitched shriek going off repeatedly.

She wasn't happy to hear that the only layer of protection she needed was to keep her body near mine so that I did not burn again.

I take heart in the fact that she cared enough about me to worry when I burned. More than that, she showed me that she sees me as *her* mate by providing for me. In the human world, I cannot hunt for her. Until I bring her to Sombra with me, I must follow her lead.

Though, after I share a meal with her, I know I must bring some of the human food back with us. It is delicious, and even if I'd prefer to sate my hunger by feasting on Sierra's cunt, it is enough that she invites me to slumber in her quarters with her when we're done with our meal.

Most of the night, she spends it paying attention to

that small glass rectangle of hers. Without her essence, I don't know what is so fascinating about it other than it's how she hunted our food for us, plus measured how large of a male I am. My mate and I already ate our food, so there's no reason for her to continue tapping it with her wee human finger, but I've already upset her enough this eve to point that out to her now.

So I stay quiet, watching her instead, waiting for some sign that she is ready to welcome me at last.

It never comes, but I'm not worried. That she trusts me enough to guard her as she slumbers is enough for me. And when Sierra finally climbs in her bedding, telling me to make myself comfortable in one of her chairs, I nod, and plop on the wood floor at the foot of her bed, ready to protect her from any predator that might find its way into her quarters.

Sombra males need only a few hours of sleep every couple of moons. Hunters need even less. I'd much prefer to watch over my Sierra. It matters not that we will have eternity together. This is our first eve, and I will do everything I can to prove myself to her.

My next challenge comes long after Sierra falls asleep in the center of her nest.

My mate is snuffling softly, her delicate snores so adorable, I choose to continue sitting with my back against her elevated bedding so that I can listen to their melody. I am content, even if I'd prefer to be curving my demon body around her.

I won't push her. That's not the way to win her trust and her affection. I'm grateful that I've already earned enough of it that she freed me from the containment circle, but with the salt and the giz perched near her bed, I'm not arrogant enough to believe she won't contain me again if I anger her.

My Sierra is lovely when she's angry, but it hurts her to be, and I will never do anything to hurt her.

I won't let anything hurt her, either.

I'm vigilant. All of my senses are on alert. My nose is so attuned to Sierra and her musk, it's all I scent. The human world itself is so pungent, I purposely search out any trace of my mate to drown it.

But my ears... I listen to her snuffles, but they're not so loud that I miss the scratching sound coming from the other side of her door.

I cock my head. I've heard scratches like that before when prey beasts in the shadows turn solid to hunt on their own, unaware that a Sombra demon lurks close by. Is that a human prey beast? I guarded Sierra to set my own mind at ease, and to take the focus off of my aching cock.

Is there truly a threat coming from inside her quarters?

I must find out.

In an instant, I switch from my demon form to my shadows so that I can meld into the darkness in her space. Crouching low, I move toward the wooden door that closes her private quarters off from the rest of her lair.

"*Mrow.*" Scratch. Scratch. Scratch. "*Mrooow.*"

It is a beast. I have never heard such a cry before, but when I use my claws to turn the door handle the way I watched Sierra do so earlier, the door pushes in and I get my first glimpse of a human prey beast.

I suck in a breath.

An ungez.

Why is there an ungez in Sierra's lair? And such a malformed one at that.

It has the same shadow fur as the ungez I am familiar with. Its tail is as thick, though its muzzle isn't as pointed. This ungez has a flatter face and larger ears, and instead of the white eyes glowing at me from out of the shadows, this creature's are mirror-like and... *green*?

An ungez is an easy prey beast to hunt. In Sombra, a lazy hunter can trap dozens easily without much effort. They are friendly, and I've seen ungez walk into a hunter's grasp instead of fleeing for its existence.

I couldn't hunt for Sierra's evening meal. This creature would be perfect to break her fast after she slumbers.

I click my claws at the ungez. "Come," I tell it. "Let me hunt you for my mate."

The strange ungez hisses at me. It opens its mouth,

showing off wee fangs and a pink tongue, before making that nose and darting past me.

Gods. This ungez is fast.

But I am faster.

I track the creature as it runs across Sierra's quarters. Because it's prey, if smarter than Sombran ungez, I expect it to launch its shadowy hide beneath her bedding. I'm prepared to launch myself directly after it, using my claw to snag it since I am without my bow or my spear.

Only the ungez is more wily than I thought. It does not disappear there.

Instead, with one graceful leap, it lands right on top of my slumbering mate.

Who, with a strange sound torn from her bountiful chest, is no longer slumbering.

SIERRA

If there's one thing I learned after a life on the road, it's that I can fall asleep anywhere. My schedule is usually so tightly packed, I'll take a few minutes' rest where I can find it. And maybe that's reckless, knocking out and leaving myself vulnerable to anyone who might be around, but you forget that I've been surrounded by security nearly my whole damn life.

What happened with Patrick Ridgefield was a fluke. It took me a while to get past him enough to function, and a whole lot of sessions with Dr. Lopez, but I finally was able to fall asleep without having nightmares of being shot in the face.

I meant to stay up last night. For one, I still hadn't heard from Billie. The groomers closed at eight, and she still wasn't home with Three by nine. I trust her, so I texted her, asking if she decided to bring Three to Connecticut with her and Trevor.

Like with Jared, there was no response. That's not too unusual. Billie is usually glued to her phone, and while Trevor doesn't seem to mind most of the time, when she's supposed to be 'off', he likes her to be 'off'. I get that and figured that was what was going on.

Even if I was worried about my cat...

Worried about the demon who not only burned his arm, but whose entire body was a fireball when I burst into my bedroom with the fire extinguisher? Nah. Dagon immediately went back to his shadowy form before I had the chance to use the extinguisher, and I got a crash course about how that will happen every time I get too far away from him.

In a way, I'm glad that it did. Once he assured me he was fine, that he didn't feel any pain once the fire went out, I was able to understand that this is just another one of those demon things he takes for granted. If he'd just told me that he'd burst into flame if I left him, I don't know if I'd have believed him.

Seeing it? Yeah. I believe him.

And that's how I ended up with a demon sleeping at the foot of my bed like an oversized guard dog.

I'm not insane enough to roll over and invite him to

join me. Putting him in the guest room was out of the question if I didn't want a repeat of the smoke detector going off. I was lucky it turned off as soon as the fire died and that we didn't have the FDNY knocking at our door.

I couldn't risk it happening again, and I told him to get comfy in a chair.

He insisted on the floor.

Dagon wanted to curl up at the foot of my bed like a pet? That weirded me out even more. I mean, I don't even treat Three like that. My baby boy has a six-level cat tree in the living room, his own bunk on the tour bus when we're on the road, and a permanent spot on top of my pillows for when he wants to join me in my room at home.

But he's still not here, and I think the whole night took a lot more out of me than I thought because I didn't argue with the demon. I just waited until Dagon took up his position at the foot of my bed before laying down myself when suddenly—

"Oof!"

I swear, I didn't even realize I was asleep until a flying furball lands on the middle of my gut, waking me up instantly as he uses me as a launching pad to disappear into the pool of pillows behind me.

The immediate disorientation makes it obvious I *was* sleeping, and for a good while, too. Long enough to be in such a deep sleep that a fifteen-pound cat landed dead center on my belly, knocking the air out of me as I got rudely ripped out of my unconsciousness.

When I realize that's what happened, I'm so confused. I mean, I'm glad Three is back and that he's not hiding. Last time we took him out of the apartment to go to the vet, he was so ticked off, he pissed in one of my Laboutin heels in revenge, then hid on the other side of the apartment for two days.

I didn't see him before I knocked out—I remember that much—but my door was closed. Unless the groomer gave Three a pair of opposable thumbs or something, how did he get in here?

And why is my cat trembling against the top of my hair?

Reaching behind me, I pet him a few times to let him know that I'm here, and that it's okay. In my experience, certain cats get the three a.m. zoomies, and while One didn't before I lost him in the break-up, my beloved Two did, and so does Three.

But that wasn't a zoomie run. If it was, he would've kept going, and I would've woken up tomorrow with a stray scratch from wherever his claws got me.

Sitting up, I peer out into the shadows—and that's when I see the two laser pointers focused on me.

What the...

Oh my God. Oh my *God*.

How did I forget that I have a demon in my room?

A demon who isn't focused on me... but, instead,

the cat that's trying to bury itself beneath my mound of pillows.

Forget sleeping. I'm wide awake now as I hop out of the bed, dashing for the nearest light switch. I turn it on, and there's Dagon in his shadows, still staring at where Three is doing his best decorative pillow impression.

"Ah," he says, drifting closer to the bed. "I see the beast. Stay there, my mate. I will hunt it for you."

Hunt my cat?

Did I get the totally wrong idea about this demon? That he's not harmless, but a cat murderer?

No!

I jump in front of the demon, throwing out my arms so that I'm blocking his path. "Leave Three alone!"

He immediately stills. "Three?" he echoes. "What is a 'three'?"

"My cat, and I'll never forgive you if you hurt him!"

"I don't want to upset you, Sierra, but I am... confused. 'Cat'. I do not know this word."

Are you kidding? Hunting around the bed, I reach into the pillows, tucking my grumpy cat against my chest. Normally, Three would bat at me and cry to be put down, but I guess coming face-to-face with a *demon* is enough to knock the sass out of even this guy.

"This is a cat. It's my pet. We don't hunt pets in my world, Dagon."

"That creature?" Dagon frowns. "I thought it was an ungez. I was going to hunt it for your morning meal."

The thought of eating my baby makes me want to hurl, and I distract myself from thinking about what might have happened to Three if he didn't wake me up when he did by wondering: what the hell is an *ungez*?

The answer comes instantly when the image of one appears in front of my mind's eye.

Huh. It's like this cat-squirrel hybrid *thing*. Apart from the bushy tail and the wispy black fur—which I bet is shadows on the ungez, similar to the demon's— they don't look anything alike. Three is way, way cuter, especially without the couple of mats near his behind he refused to let Billie or me brush out before his trip to the groomers.

"He is *not* an ungez. And he's not food, either. His name is Three. He lives here with us, and he's a very good boy."

The demon furrows his brow, even more confused than before.

After a moment, he holds up three massive fingers. "Three?"

I nod. And, yeah, I know it's not the most conventional name for a cat. A lot of people think that, despite being a multiple award-winning songwriter, I sucked when it came to coming up with names for my pets and that I just named them after what number cat they are. That's not true.

Though, to be fair, the truth is a little bit more embarrassing to admit...

Ah, well. "Yeah. I got my first cat from an ex-boyfriend. One."

Jared named her as a 'joke' because every Thr33-peat song began with 'One-Two-Three' before we started singing. Tandy was 'One', Billie was 'Two', and as the youngest, I was 'Three'. When I asked him why the kitten wasn't called 'Three', he said it would be stupid to start with 'Three' instead of 'One'.

Then I found out he was fucking Tandy on the side a couple of months later, and that made a whole lot more sense.

I was attached to One, but seeing the Siamese cat brought back all the old hurt. It was worse when Jared demanded custody of her when we broke up. I had no choice. One was a gift, but he paid for her, microchipped her in his name and his mom's address, and was on all the papers when she got fixed.

I had no choice. I had to give her up, and was only happy about it when I found out Mrs. Turner got to keep One instead of Jared giving her to Tandy as a consolation prize when Thr33peat broke up, so did they, and Jared moved on to his next target.

Then Billie got me Two, and she was mine in every way until Patrick fucking Ridgefield.

If I'd known what he had done to my baby, I never would've adopted Three with Billie. But she insisted because I was so heartbroken over losing another cat, and we basically became helicopter parents to the most spoiled long-haired kitty in Manhattan.

After Ridgefield confessed to nabbing Two with the help of our petsitter, we became even worse.

And Dagon wanted me to *eat* him?

I tighten my hold on Three. "After I lost One, it just made sense to go with Two in honor of a friend, and, well, this special guy is Three. We. Don't. Eat. Three. Understand?"

He nods, but honestly?

I don't think Dagon heard anything past 'ex-boyfriend'.

"You had another mate? Before me? Where is he? I will challenge him for you now."

"Well, I'm not a virgin, if that's what you're asking with 'other mate'. But I'm single now. There's no one for you to challenge, so chill, okay?"

Again, I don't think English is translating into his demon language as precisely as he hopes.

"I am a Sombra demon. I am made of fire and shadows, so I'm not as chilled as you are. But I think I understand. You have mated before, but you no longer have a male. Is that what you are telling me, Sierra?"

Oh... the way his deep voice rumbles my name sends shivers down my spine.

Wait. What was he asking?

It takes a second, but I nod. Three yowls softly and, taking pity on him, I lay his bulk back down on the pillows.

He disappears, leaving only his freshly trimmed rump and swishing tail in the air.

I turn toward Dagon again. "Yup," I say daringly. "Is that a problem?"

"No. It is better that at least one of us knows the proper way to mate. You can show me how you like it. As for not having a male... it would matter not if you did. The gods have given you to me, my mate. I am your male now."

I blink.

Okay, then.

THE DEMON SWEARS HE WILL NEVER TRY TO EAT THREE again. I want to believe him, but I'd rather not test the theory. So, instead of going back to bed, I carry Three into the bathroom with me, tell Dagon to stay behind, and take a quick shower where I can keep my eye on my pet.

Once we're clean and Three is yowling for his breakfast, I carry him out to the kitchen. He gets two cans of wet food as an apology for both the groomer and Dagon. I dish them into the same bowl, then hand it to the demon.

"Are you feeding me again, my mate?"

I snort. "Not for you, buddy. That's for Three. Give it to him. He'll forgive a lot if you give him wet food. Two cans? He might just be your best friend."

"Ah... and you want your creature to be fond of your male, yes?"

No. I want the demon who's crashing in my place not to eat my cat. "Sure."

Dagon places the bowl down. Three eyes him suspiciously.

Dagon scoots it closer to the cat. "Eat. Please."

Three approaches the bowl cautiously. Unlike me, he can't understand Dagon's demon language; though, to be far, he probably doesn't understand English, either... but he is completely food-motivated. He sniffs the mush, and when it seems to pass his muster, he starts to scarf it down.

That taken care of, I place an order for Dagon and me from the local deli.

It's faster than dinner was. I'm just throwing on my usual wig and glasses, ignoring the questioning look coming from my 'mate' as I put on the disguise.

I wish I didn't have to. If Billie was here, I wouldn't. But as much as I trust the Dorado team, my petsitter betraying me proves that you really can't trust *anyone*. What if one of the front desk guys gets bribed to let someone else up?

Better to be safe than sorry. If they think they're going to see Whiskey Rose and get a brunette in glasses instead, maybe they'll go on their merry way without bothering me.

As the elevator door opens, I turn behind me to remind Dagon to go to another room so that no one sees him. I'm impressed by how quick he was because he's already gone, but once I have our breakfast... he's still missing.

"Dagon? Where did you go?"

I sense him near. Like when you grab a staticky piece of clothing from your closet and get zapped, there's a constant electrical shock passing between us that I've noticed since my rude awakening this morning. Like, I can *feel* him near me... but I don't see him.

Did he actually leave *leave*? He told me that he couldn't conjure a way back to his demon world while our bond was unsettled. Did he figure out how? Or did he decide to explore the furthest reaches of the apartment that he can make it to without burning while I was busy collecting the food from Ralph?

I hear his voice before I see him.

"I am here, Sierra."

"Where?"

There.

Whoa.

I swear, he wasn't there. It wasn't that he was his shadows, either. He was *gone*—and then he wasn't.

Fading back into existence, he goes from light to dark in a few heartbeats.

"Holy shit. You can disappear?"

"I can control my shadows, yes."

I don't get it—but I want to. With the hand not holding onto our breakfast, I gesture at him. "Do that again."

He fades so quickly, he goes from his inky black shadows to nothingness in seconds.

Only this time I was paying close attention. His opacity has gone down to zero, but if I squint, I can just about see him. There's a vague Dagon-like outline in front of me, hovering off of the floor.

So he didn't disappear. Not completely.

"Okay. You can come back now." As soon as he does, I say, "I thought you only had two forms. When you're big and red—"

"My demon form, yes."

Right. "And when all I can see is darkness and your glowing eyes."

"When I am in my shadows."

"Uh-huh. But what was that? What did you just do?"

Dagon frowns. "Don't you know? It's in my essence."

Yeah, and I've purposely been blocking that off as much as I can since last night.

"It's fine. If you don't want to answer me, you don't have to. I was just curious."

He crosses the small amount of space between us in two oversized steps. Before I can guess how bold he's about to be, my demon slides his claws through my hair, cupping the back of my head with his palm as he rubs the pad of his thumb along the height of my cheek.

"Anything you wish to learn, I will tell you. I like that you want to get to know your male. If you'd prefer to learn from me, I will teach you." His heated gaze drops to my lips, roving over the shape of the bow. "As you've already taught me so much about your world in the short time you've called me to your side."

My stomach twists, but I'm not nervous. Not nauseous or hungry, either.

Fuck. I'm suddenly so attracted to him, it almost *hurts*—and what the hell is *that* about?

I swallow, then turn away, hustling to the living room. "Come on. Let's eat in here again."

"As you wish, my mate."

I start dishing out the order. As I do, I realize something else.

Dagon is a big demon. I'm going to have to start ordering double for the amount of food his size must need, but he doesn't complain as I pass over the container of steak and eggs I ordered for him.

With his fixation on hunting and meat, I figured this was something he might like.

He does. He uses his claws to slice the steak into chunks, then pierces the meat to eat it. The eggs he scoops up with a spoon, smirking a little when he notices my surprise.

Against my better judgment, I return the smirk and start to eat my omelet.

I'm not paying attention to him as he eats after that. The flash of attraction from before has me lost in my own thoughts, though I do notice he goes through his steak a lot faster than the eggs.

Then, about halfway through my omelet, he says one word: "Mist."

Huh?

I glance over at him.

"I'm just finishing answering your question from before. Mist... that's what we call it when we fade. Rain is not common in my corner of Sombra. I live on the edge, near the ash fields in the village of Caol. We see it fall maybe once a year, but there is still mist. It's a Sombra demon's way of melting into the shadows around them. For some, it's a defense mechanism. For hunters like your male, I can disappear so completely that the prey don't see me until they are meat.

"But not Three," he says solemnly. Grabbing a piece of steak from his container with his claws, he drops it to the floor. "Three is a fellow hunter. I can sense that about him. We will get along nicely."

Three is a lazy cat who belongs to a wealthy, famous superstar who spoils him rotten.

But even I don't give him human food straight from my plate—and now I know why the steak is almost gone.

I smile. Maybe I won't have to worry about these two guys after all.

SIERRA

After breakfast, I put on *Jessica's Journey* for him.

Is it conceited of me? To entertain a demon from another world by putting on a movie that I starred in?

Probably.

Dagon's never seen a movie. The vibe I get about Sombra is that it's part hunter/gatherer society, part magically advanced universe. They don't have the tech that we do in the human world because they have no need for it.

Some things are obviously universal. Houses. Bathrooms. Spoons, I found out. Clothes, like how Dagon covers his dick up with shadows once he realized that he might've been a bit too forward, flashing me the way he did.

But movies? Music? All the things I'm known for and that I'm actually good at?

They mean nothing to him, and that means—for my own pride—I delight in sharing them with the demon.

It takes Dagon about five minutes into the film to finally understand that someone hasn't used magic to shrink me and put me behind the glass screen; at least, that's how he explains it. Once he does, he enjoys watching the story for the most part, though he keeps referring to my character as 'Sierra' instead of 'Jessica' because, well, to him, that *is* Sierra.

His one issue with it?

Aiden, the role played by Colin Mathers, my handsy co-star.

I forgot about how romantic *Jessica's Journey* gets. It's supposed to be a road trip film about three friends, with a hint of a 'coming of age' twist to it. Colin's character is the friend 'Jessica' left behind at the beginning of said journey, but he loves her so much, he meets her halfway through the trip to confess his love.

Dagon... yeah. He wasn't the biggest fan of watching the two characters on screen when they have their big love scene at a Motel 6.

Whoops.

As soon as he sees it, he starts grumbling under his

breath. His claws rip into the cushion of the settee we're sitting on, but I pretend not to notice. His eyes are red, but if they could change color, they'd be fucking green with the amount of envy creeping its way toward me down this tie stretching between us— our bond, as he thinks of it—while I watch him watch *me* out of the corner of my eye.

I can't help it. Seeing him be so jealous of another guy kissing me... it's fucking hot as hell. It's also a boost to an already overinflated ego I probably don't need. And then, because he seemed so interested in the 'movie', I hit him with the big guns.

I play him my first album on the old record player we keep in the living room because I've always liked it. I have all my records on vinyl, and there's something about using the old-fashioned technology to play it that really makes me feel like a proper singer and not a manufactured pop star.

Not that there's anything wrong with that. My issues with my career stem from the fact that I'm in my thirties now, and so many people still see me as a nine-teen-year-old Whiskey Rose, crying over a douchebag who cheated on her.

"Heart Barely Used" is the reason why I became a superstar. I still enjoy all of my records because each one is personal to me, but to really introduce Dagon to Whiskey Rose, I need to start from the beginning and work my way through to the end.

And that lasts about four songs into *Whiskey Rose*, my debut, before I get antsy and throw on "Heart Barely Used". It's the last track, and the first song that I released—and wrote.

When the song finishes—and a small smile curves my lips as nineteen-year-old Sierra ends it with *in the spotlight, I'll shine with a heart barely used*—I can't help myself any longer: I ask Dagon his opinion.

He covers my hand with one of his massive ones.

"Your sounds are lovely, Sierra," he says, and his words ring with truth. Truth and *pride*. "If it pleases you, I'd love to hear more."

My smile kicks up a little higher.

I know I'm a fan-fucking-tastic singer. That's not even me being cocky. It's just fact. I wouldn't have the career I do if I didn't know how to sing. Billie likes to say I can sing "Twinkle, Twinkle, Little Star" and it'll get a million streams overnight, and I am vain enough to agree.

He likes my sounds. Cool.

But that's not what I'm fishing for here, demon.

I scoot closer to him. "What about the actual song? I mean, the words."

People always think that I'm just the pretty face, the sexy body, and the voice. My super fans all know which songs off of my self-titled debut were forced on me by the producers and the record label, but I managed to sneak one or two on it that I wrote myself, including "Heart Barely Used". By my third album, I had enough pull that every single song was mine.

Too many critics wrote me off as a one-hit wonder. To be fair, my sophomore album bombed in comparison to my debut, so I get it. It didn't matter that my sophomore album still sold more copies than any other out that year. Mine didn't beat my previous numbers, and that's all that counted to the suits.

My third album was my shot to show the world who Whiskey Rose really is. I had wanted to call it *Sierra*, a bid toward shedding my pop star idol image once I hit twenty-five, but I didn't have enough pull for *that*.

Is it a surprise that they took one of the most well-known lines from my first hit—*in this world of stardust* —to title the album *Stardust* to remind my fans who I was, who the powers that be sold as Whiskey Rose? Nah. But with my fifth album planned for next year, I'm still holding out hope I can finally call that one *Sierra* instead.

As I wait a bit breathlessly for his answer, I have to ask myself if it really does matter if my demon knows that I wrote the words he heard me singing on the record?

The answer is undeniably *yes*.

I don't know for sure *why* it does—or if his insistence that he's my true love is finally getting to me at last—but it seems... important somehow that *Dagon* believes I'm more than my raspy set of pipes and the babydoll smile programmed into me from the time I was a kid.

I love singing. I always have, and I'm sure I always will. Before my injury, I used to sing around the apartment all the time. Billie doesn't mind; though she gave up show biz years ago to work behind the scenes, she still loves to sing, too, and sometimes we'll do silly duets together in the living room.

When Dagon smiles at me and says, "They are brilliant, but so are you, my mate," I almost want to sing again for the first time since California.

WE DON'T SEE THREE DURING THE MOVIE OR WHEN I play my debut album for Dagon. Miraculously, though, he waltzes into the living room right in the middle of our lunch.

He parks his furry rump beneath the antique coffee table. He must think I don't see the great black lump as he sticks his head out, eating the pieces of chicken that Dagon offers him.

I'd expected that this time. And while I got chicken parmesan for Dagon to try, I ordered a piece of grilled chicken on the side and conveniently mentioned that red sauce is bad for cats, but plain chicken is okay in moderation.

A piece of plain chicken for Three, a chunk of sauce and cheese for Dagon... and Sierra is smiling into her Caesar salad.

Only once we finished up our lunch and I threw the containers into the delivery bags does my cat—who we adopted five years ago, and who has Whiskey Rose herself personally cleaning his shit box—finally deign to remember that I exist.

He notices my lap is empty and walks right onto it before immediately turning around and putting his furry ass in my face.

Thanks, Three. No, really.

Dagon grins. "Ah. You've been claimed by this creature."

"You and your obsession with claiming," I tease. Three starts kneading me through my leggings. Thankfully, the groomers clipped his nails so I'll only end up with a few scratches instead of the heavy kitty ripping my thighs open... and, yet, I love him anyway.

I scratch his pointed little chin with one hand, his rump with the other.

Three begins to purr. I return Dagon's grin. "I told you. He's my pet."

"Your cat."

I nod. "Yup. Same thing, demon."

"Pet," he says, trying the word out in English. I guess there really is no translation in Sombran for what Three is, and he proves that by asking, "What precisely does that mean?"

I snort. "Well, when you have a pet, you don't let a hunter turn him into breakfast for one."

I tried to be good-natured about it because I accepted that it was one big miscommunication, and that Dagon only wanted to 'hunt' Three to feed me. Still, I'm not about to let him live this down so soon.

And then he does something that makes me second-guess that: he addresses Three personally.

Dagon bows his head in the cat's direction. "I humbly apologize again, creature—"

"Three."

"Yes. Three. You are a fierce beast and not prey. I will remember that. I vow it. No one will hunt you while I am here."

Three stares at Dagon for a moment. With a twitch of his ears, he yawns, then jumps off of my lap and onto the hardwood floor. His tail goes straight up in the air, Three-speak for: you're forgiven, peasant.

Good one, Dagon. No clue if Three understands how solemnly my demon means that vow, but it's the thought that counts.

Damn it.

"Okay," I say, treating his question a little more seriously now. "Pets. Well, when you have a pet, you feed him. You play with him. You take care of him." *You play rock-paper-scissors with Billie over who will clean the litter box while Gladys is away...* "You love him. You stroke his fur—"

"I would be your 'pet' if you allowed it."

Oh. Okay. Don't know where that came from, but... "Why's that?"

"I want you to run your fingers through my hair." His voice drops, going husky as he gives me another of those fervent, unblinking stares. "I want your mouth pressed to my skin the way you do the creature's shadows."

"You mean, a kiss?"

Dagon's red eyes flare brightly at my not-so-innocent question.

Ah. It's not an exact translation—the image that pops into my brain straight out of Dagon's is of two demons rubbing their horns together—but the shot of lust slamming into my chest tells me that he wants to rub more than his horns on *me.*

Still, I have to ask. "Do you know what a kiss is?"

"Yes." He glances away. "I've seen the duke and his mate put their mouths together. I've always wondered what it would be like to do that with the female meant for me."

Another straight shot of *need* comes barreling down the line stretching between us, so powerful that I clench my thighs together for a little pressure.

The female meant for him...

Me.

I lay my hand on his bicep. He goes still under my touch, as though afraid to react in case I draw away from him.

I don't. Actually, I move *closer*.

"Do you want me to press my mouth to your skin like I do Three," I ask, running my fingers lightly over his fever-hot flesh, "or to your mouth?"

Dagon shudders, then grates out, "I want you to do to me what you did to the male in your 'movie'. Like the duke and his mate."

A kiss on the lips, then.

No.

It's a French kiss in *Jessica's Journey*. I remember that vividly because Colin had a tendency to drool a little after the fifth or so take, and I had to walk around with cinnamon gum in my costume pocket to offer him before we got started.

Hmm. I wonder what Dagon will taste like.

Only one way to find out...

I was almost afraid that kissing Dagon would be like sticking my tongue in an ashtray. It's the fiery nature of his demon, and the memory of 'barbecue' that filled my room after I summoned him. I'm pleased to be wrong about that.

There's a whisper of chicken and sauce from our lunch. As I nibble on his thick bottom lip before slipping my tongue into his mouth, careful to avoid his fangs as I stroke my much cooler tongue against his super warm one... I get heat. I get fire. I get something spicy, and all of it together as I grip his chin so that I can kiss him even deeper.

At first, Dagon doesn't move. He lets me do what I want to him, including putting my tongue in his mouth which—according to his surprise—he totally isn't expecting. Then, right when I slant my mouth, allowing myself to breathe through my nose better as I continue to kiss him, he cradles the back of my head with his hand.

And then he kisses *me*.

When I finally pull myself away from him, it's not because it's awkward or it's messy. It is, but in all the best ways; the messy part since it's actually not awkward at all. But when I realize I'm seconds away from climbing into his lap and rubbing myself all over him?

Yeah. I need a little distance—and probably another cold shower.

His gaze burns brightly as he darts out his tongue, swiping it over his bottom lip, leaving them shiny and oh so tempting.

He rumbles deep in his chest. "Thank you, my mate. For your 'kiss', and for... everything."

I want to remind him that I'm not his mate. That I can't be. That what just passed between us was a mistake, but it would be a lie, wouldn't it?

Instead, I pat him on the chest.

"Don't mention it, demon."

DAGON IS A PERFECT GENTLEMAN.

Despite our kissing lesson, we don't go any farther than that. I confess, I might've been testing both my resolve and his by allowing him to sleep in my bed instead of my floor, but the more time I spend with him —and the more I learn about him from his essence—it's harder and harder to justify treating him like a predator.

And if I doubted my motives, I felt a whole lot better when Three followed us into my bedroom when we were getting ready to settle in after a long day of movie-watching, album-listening, and stuffing our faces with so much food, I'm sure the guys at the desk downstairs are wondering what's going on with me.

I thought my cat might want to keep his distance, maybe take advantage of sleeping in Billie's bed since she's gone, but after the way Dagon shared his steak at breakfast and his chicken at lunch, he already had Three in the palm of his hand.

By the time I caught him sneaking Three some crumbled sausage from our pizza dinner, I'm pretty sure my cat was beginning to like Dagon more than me.

I'll have to put a stop to that tomorrow. When the

demon is gone, I don't want Three to get used to being fed people food—especially since I won't be able to explain to Billie how he suddenly picked up the taste for it. But, for now, he deserves a tiny treat after nearly being *hunted* this morning, and I like seeing Dagon and Three getting along.

And they are. Instead of cozying up in Billie's bed or his cat tree, Dagon sprawls out at the end of the bed with us.

Part of me thinks that the greedy kitty just wants to bask in the warmth coming from the demon. The other part? I sneak a picture of the two of them together, then store it in a private folder on my phone so that I can remember Dagon when he has to leave.

Because he will. He wants something from me that I can't give, and—kiss or no kiss—I haven't changed my mind about this just being a weekend thing before he has to figure out a way to go.

But that's Monday morning Sierra's problem. Saturday night Sierra? Against her better judgment— or maybe because of it—she curls up with her warm demon and her purring cat and has the best night of sleep she's had in *weeks*.

Dagon doesn't try anything. The demon even angles his hips back so I don't accidentally make contact with the erection he can't quite conceal even beneath his shadowy coverings. He's obviously still intent on 'wooing' me, of trying to convince me to be his mate, but he's doing everything at my speed.

Like I said, perfect gentleman.

If only I could say the same for myself…

I don't want to lead him on. I don't initiate anything, either, though I really, really want to. I only know about the erection because, when he angled his hips back, I wickedly scooted a little closer, knowing he would never refuse me.

I claim it's because I'm cold, that I need his warmth, too… and that's part of it.

And the other part is that I'm a big, stinking liar who is way more attracted to the demon than I have any right to be.

But because I was so close to Dagon while we were sleeping, it's easy to notice that something isn't right on Sunday morning. I already learned from his essence that Dagon doesn't sleep very often, so it's nice to wake up first, watching the ridges over his nose wrinkling slightly as he snores a bit. His hair is spread out over my pillow, his shoulder, even my forearm, and his breath is blowing in my face.

It's cool.

What?

I lay my hand on his shoulder. That's cold, too.

What's going on?

I shake him. With his instincts, his eyes snap open immediately, instantly aware.

"Sierra. What is it? Are you well?"

I'm fine.

"Yeah. What about you? Are you okay?" I place the back of my hand on his forehead. I curse under my breath, snatching my hand away from his skin. "Holy shit, Dagon. You're like *ice*."

He blinks, his eyes dimmer than they have been. He gives me another fang-filled grin, and when he says, "Of course I'm well, my mate," I know that Dagon has lied to me for the first time.

I just don't know what to do about that.

DAGON

The mate sickness is upon me.

I had hoped that I would be strong enough to withstand it. In Sombra, the mate sickness occurs when one who is Other doesn't accept the bond. The gods will have their way, though, and if their fated pairs refuse to admit there is a tie, the fever reminds them that it exists.

I know it does. I also know that my Sierra is human. Even with my essence, she doesn't understand quite what it means to be the one true mate to a demon. It is my duty as her male to teach her, and if I must wait for her to choose me, then that is what I will do.

The gold moon is a deadline imposed by the duke

on the rare occasion a demon finds his mate in the legendary world of mortals. The deadline doesn't exist in my world, but we are not in Sombra, are we? And until I bond Sierra to me—or release her from our tie—I cannot return home.

Thankfully, the gold moon is still a cycle away. I have more time to woo my mate than some of my fellow demons, and already I've made some progress with Sierra. She hasn't screamed in fright again, and once I apologized for trying to hunt her personal creature, she even provided meals for *me*.

I have no doubt that she is my one true mate. In time, she will agree... but with the mate sickness creeping up my spine, icing out my veins... the chill dimming my gaze... I have run out of time.

The mate sickness is upon me—and as much as I hope I can beat it, now that I've lost my fire and I have no essence to warm me up, I am in trouble.

If Sierra had gifted me her essence instead of keeping it, the chill never would've taken hold. Not that I fault her for being careful. Sharing her essence with her male is a gift, and she's kept her guard up every time we've touched. Even now, as she brushes her hand against my brow, I sense the whisper-thin bond between us and my undeniable need for her, and that is all.

That is my fault. I haven't done enough to earn her trust or her affection just yet. I will continue to try, and pray to the gods that I can resist the mate sickness until I do.

There is only one thing I can do at this time. Hoping Sierra doesn't use my essence to tell that I'm purposely concealing my state from her, I pat her hand gently, then rise up from my post at the side of her bedding.

Since appearing in my mate's impressive quarters, I've been aroused more often than not. I've grown used to having a cockstand, though there's something different about this one. It aches as my sac goes tight, and I realize that I'm ready to spill my seed from that single pat alone.

My shadows are woven around my lower form, hiding my hard cock from her curious stare. Since I revealed it to her, I've caught my mate glancing at my shadows as though she's interested in seeing it again.

I'm more than happy to share my body with Sierra; after all, it's belonged to her from the moment I recognized her as my mate. The mate sickness makes that impossible. Just the weight of her naked stare would have me exploding.

I must control myself. A good hunter knows when to react and when to retreat. With my hands curling in on themselves, forming a fist as my claws stab into the meat of my palm in a bid to keep that control, I murmur that I need to relieve myself.

Sierra frowns. "Uh, yeah. Sure. I showed you where the bathroom was, right?"

She did the morning before. In her large quarters, there are multiple toilets, and keeping to my shadow form so that my cockstand isn't as obvious, I glide to the nearest one.

This toilet is kept in a small space off of Sierra's personal sleeping area. A wooden door separates both parts of her quarters. Usually, I wouldn't shut myself off from my mate, but with the instinct to get her under me suddenly consuming, I must put as much distance between us as the bond will allow.

I'm stretching the limits as I shift shapes, going solid as I park my feet on the floor of her 'bathroom'. My skin has lost some of its richness, fading slightly as the mate sickness continues to chill me to my bones.

The only relief for the sickness comes from an intimate touch. I cannot ask my mate for her to stroke me. I would push her away if I rushed her into mating— and I refuse.

Instead, I take my own cock in hand.

Over the centuries, I've found pleasure in tugging on my cock whenever I imagined what my mate would be. Whether she would be a demoness from Sombra or another realm, such as Brielle or Soleil, or—after meeting Susanna—if she would be a human female of my own... I would spare a moment from my hunts to stroke roughly until my seed was spurting all over my grip.

It was a tiny release, just enough pleasure to remind me what I was longing for. It's been many cycles since I've done so, and though I've been erect since arriving in the human world, I was waiting until my mate wanted to lay her fingers along my shaft.

One day, it will be her hand on me. For now, I make quick work of my erection, swallowing my moan as my cock releases its seed into the toilet. Remembering how Sierra showed how the flusher works in the human world, I send the water away, then use the sink to wash my hands and my claws.

Better.

***

Sierra is sitting on the couch in her living quarters. Three is perched on her lap, purring softly while his flashing green eyes are narrowed into slits, watching me.

Can the creature sense the return of the mate sickness?

I've excused myself to the toilet three times since the 'movie' began. The last time, no matter how roughly I stroked my cock, it refused to do anything but throb. I've heard of something like this happening before. The longer the mate sickness lasts, the more it becomes a true sickness. Despite the chill, sweat has beaded along my brow. My stomach is cramping. My tongue has gone dry, and I cup some of the water from the claw-washing station to swallow.

It's useless. The only thing that will bring me relief is an intimate touch from my mate. It's already been two moons since our bond was triggered when I gave her my essence, and apart from when she put her mouth to mine, teaching me of her 'kiss', none of our fleeting touches have been intimate.

I want so badly to see if she is interested in giving me another one. I don't. It would be too tempting, and she is so cozy, curled up with her creature. With *Three*.

When she was showing me that 'movie' she was in with that other male, I noticed how her wee feet were even chillier than I am now. I used my warmth to make her comfortable then. I cannot do that now—not with the mate sickness stealing it from me—though I did retrieve some of her bedding from her quarters.

Sierra is snuggled under it, with Three on top of her lap. The last time I returned from the toilet, struggling to hide both my raw cockstand and my frustration at how badly I need my mate's touch, she smiled at me and offered the edge of the blanket for me to share.

It's a small sign of affection from my guarded mate, and I treasured it. Now? I'm even more grateful as my cock twitches, demanding someone pay attention to it.

Since I refuse to rush my mate, that leaves *me*.

My mate is watching her 'movie'. So engrossed by what the even tinier humans are doing on her rectangle—her 'television'—she doesn't notice as I dip my hand beneath the blanket, wrapping my fist around my shaft.

And then I give it a tentative stroke... and she notices *that*.

Sierra's gaze slides over to me. "Dagon?"

I stiffen, and not just my poor cock. "Yes, my mate?"

"What are you doing over there?"

A lump lodges in my throat. My mate asked me a direct question. I... I cannot deceive her.

Throwing the blanket away from my lap, I show her the way my hand is wrapped around my cock.

Her eyes widen. "Are you jerking off over there?"

Jerking off... the translation to Sombran isn't quite right, but it's close enough that I understand what she's asking. Ah. Sierra wants to know if I'm stroking my cock until release.

"No."

She snorts. "I'd say your hands are in your pants, but you don't really wear pants, do you?"

My mate is not wrong. Many of the villagers in Sombra wear woven coverings when they stay in their solid demon forms. For those of us who switch to our shadows frequently, we find our modesty in creating a covering from a thicker layer of shadows in either shape.

That's what I've done in the human world. They're easy to conjure and banish, even though I am a hunter, not a mage. For Sierra's comfort, I've made sure to keep my lower form covered... but with the fabric blanket shielding me from her, I'd released them.

I start to conjure them again, only pausing when she shakes her head.

"No, no. It's okay. You do you, Dagon. I don't care if you want to get off. Just don't stain my settee."

I frown. Unless the mate sickness is interfering with my bond, the emotions I sense coming from Sierra... it's a mixture of amusement and *lust*?

Taking in a deep breath, my heart stutters in my chest as I catch her musk on the breeze. She may protest that she is not my true mate, but in the presence of my cockstand, her body is readying itself for me again.

I know better than to point that out. Instead, I'm grateful that she is at least attracted to my demon body —and my cock.

Her tongue darts out, dabbing her bottom lip as I stroke my cock from root to tip.

"I am sorry," I tell her. "I know you told me you weren't interested in mating. But..." I shudder out a breath, knowing the time has come to be honest with her. "It is the mate sickness."

"I knew something was up when you kept running off to the bathroom. I mean, demon biology might be different from humans, but six times in two hours? Either human food was giving you the runs, or something else was going on. And considering—"

"Considering?" I echo.

Sierra shakes her head, laying a hand on Three's fuzzy back when the motion disturbs the wee creature. "Don't worry about that. Mate sickness, huh? What's that?"

"If you search my essence, you will know."

"Or you can tell me and I won't have to see things you probably don't want me to."

"I will tell you anything you desire to know, my mate—"

"Not your mate," she says quickly, interjecting.

Ah, but she is. And if my suspicions are true... if Sierra has been feeling an echo of my mate sickness since I came down with the chill... then our bond is growing stronger the more time we spend together. If that's so, then my suffering will be worth it when my mate finally welcomes me into her arms.

That is not now. So, because she asked me a question, I will answer it.

"The mate sickness triggers a need to mate when a bond is in place, but it has not been finalized. I'm still in control," I say hurriedly before Sierra can fear that I might burrow my cock into her cunt by force. No matter how the sickness affects me, I would end my existence before I ever took something from my mate that she did not freely give. "If you prefer, I will return to your nearest toilet and pleasure myself in private."

To my surprise, Sierra isn't afraid. Unless I am wrong, she's *intrigued*.

"I knew something was up with you when your head felt like ice. Mate sickness, huh? I guess a shot of Dayquil or some Ricolas won't help you, huh?"

Daykwill? Rickolah? More words that do not have a counterpart in Sombran. Assuming they are aids that help when a human has fallen ill, I shake my head. "The only relief when one suffers from the mate sickness is an intimate touch."

She jerks her chin at me, her honey eyes vibrant and alive. "From your hand?"

If only. But the gods are determined to see their fated pairs join together, and a single touch from Sierra would banish my sickness far more effectively than countless strokes from my own.

I don't tell her that. To do so would be to make my mate feel as though she must choose between touching me when she doesn't want to, or allowing the sickness to worsen.

I don't tell her that—and I don't have to.

As though she's delved into my essence enough to learn what I know about the mate sickness, Sierra *knows*.

This time, her adorable pink tongue swipes along her bottom lip. With a soft push to Three's hindquarters, she eases the creature off of her lap. Three shakes out his fur, trotting off behind the couch as Sierra inches her way closer to me.

Her hand is suddenly hovering over my lap. My cock twitches, eager to feel her soft skin against it.

I suck in a breath. "My mate?"

"You didn't answer me, demon." Sierra smiles wickedly, and just the curve of her lips showing off her blunt teeth is enough for me to produce a drop of seed on the tip of my cock. "Is it your hand that will help relieve your *mate* sickness?"

She wiggles her fingers. "Or mine?"

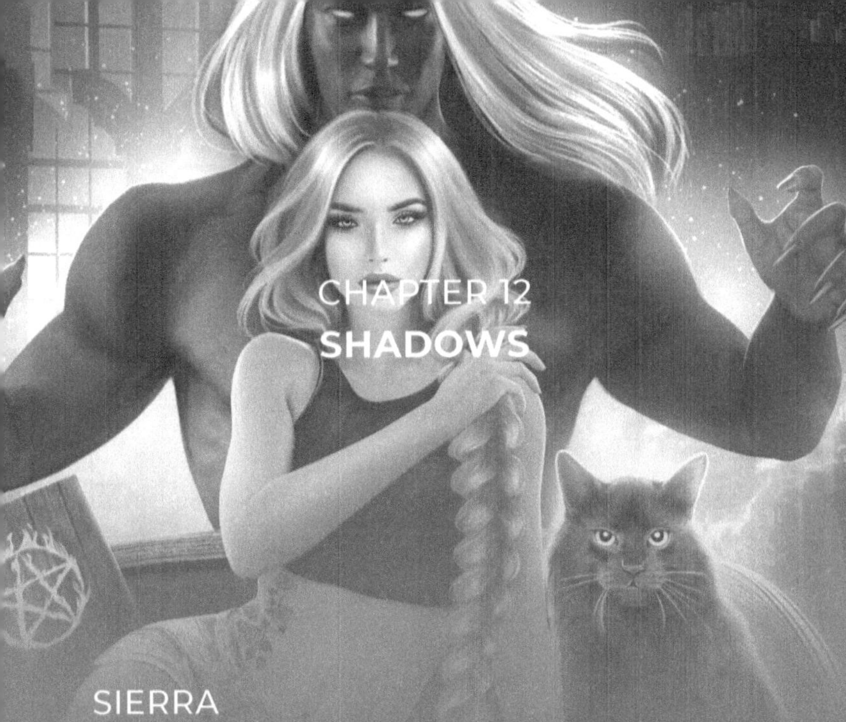

CHAPTER 12
SHADOWS

SIERRA

Oh, boy. I'm playing with fire right now—and I *like* it.

Thanks to his essence, I already knew that Dagon was fiending for me. That's part of the whole 'mate' gig. He's spent five hundred years waiting to get lucky, but because my ferocious-looking demon is a growly sweetheart deep down, he'd rather sneak off to the bathroom to rub one out than admit that he's dying for me to touch him.

I started to get suspicious this morning when I slapped my hand on his forehead and it felt like touching an ice cube. Unless he'd been feverish all along only for the fever to break last night, something was wrong.

Of course he denied it. A guy is a guy, right? He'd rather pretend he was fine than admit to me that he might be coming down with some kind of demon sickness.

And he did. Thanks to the two of us being mates, but not *bonded* mates, he's not doing so well.

I've given up on acting like we're not somehow connected. Between the strange flashes of Dagon's life that keep filling my head and the way I sense *his* emotions more than mine sometimes, there's definitely something going on here.

So I'm his mate. According to Dagon, an intimate touch should be enough to take the edge off.

If it was any other guy telling me that, I'd think he was just after a quick handjob and figured this was the best way to get one. Not Dagon. I might not be diving into his essence on purpose, but enough of it keeps eking out for me to know that he wouldn't have confessed his problem if I didn't kind of, sort of pull it out of him.

Not like I didn't already guess. Like I said, I suspected something was up. This bond we have might not be finalized yet because I haven't promised him forever—because, well, I can't—but remember the whole 'sensing his emotions' thing?

When lust hits him hard, it does a doozy on me. He might be the one who keeps disappearing to the bathroom, but I'm the one who's left squirming in her seat.

Is this what he means by mate sickness? Do I have it, too?

It would be so, so easy to blame my attraction to Dagon on that. *Oh, sorry, I had the mate sickness. I couldn't control myself...* God, even in my mind, I sound just like Jared when I say shit like that.

I can control myself. I don't do anything I don't want to... and right now? I really, really want to get a firm grip on his erection, especially when—to my delight—he produces a bead of precome on the tip, already so close to coming just from my offer.

I'll touch him. To help his mate sickness, to do something about mine... ah, who am I kidding? I don't even think I have this sickness. If anything, it's an echo of what Dagon is feeling mixed with the need I've been feeling for days now.

I wanted sex before I met Dagon. Since I summoned him to New York, my body has only grown more desperate for it. And while it's probably too soon to say fuck it and, you know, fuck *him,* I don't see any reason why I can't stroke him off if he's interested.

But, first, I need Dagon to let me know that he is.

Wiggling my fingers some more, I wait to see how he'll respond.

He's solid now. When he's in his demon form, he seems impossibly larger, and that goes double for his hard-on. Part of me doesn't even want to think about him trying to fit himself in my body, while the other part is like... you know what? That might be fun to try.

Dagon takes a deep breath, exhaling roughly after holding it for a beat. When he does, he leans back against the settee, widening his legs so that I have complete access to him.

"A mate's touch will ease the sickness," he admits at last. "But if you don't want to—"

Sorry, demon. I want.

I want very much.

I try wrapping my hand around his shaft, whistling under my breath when I can't even touch my fingers all the way around. Shit. There's still about an inch gap between the tips. That's how thick he is.

Dagon shutters his eyes, throwing his back at my first touch. "*Sierra...*"

Hey. If he likes that, he's gonna love this.

I stroke him. It's rough. He might be a little big for me to handle even like this, and I use my second hand for a little leverage to get some friction going. Pausing only to lick my palm, hoping some moisture will help, I squeeze Dagon, my grin widening as he groans.

"What's the matter, demon? Hasn't anyone ever touched you like this?"

Eyes opening to mere slits, Dagon gives a jerky shake of his head as he peers down at me. "You are the only female who has ever even seen my cock."

Really?

I keep one hand on his dick. The other dips beneath it, playing with his hairless balls. They're both firm and warm to the touch, and I only hope that means his mate sickness is starting to fade.

He starts to rumble deep in his chest, almost like a purr.

I rub my thumb over the crown, gathering the moisture there before stroking him again. "What's that? No pretty demoness got the chance to play with you before that spell dragged you to my world?"

Dagon tenses at the same time as a pretty human woman with long dark hair skitters across my mind's eye.

My smile dips.

Damn it. I've been doing everything I can to block off the memories he planted into my head when I first brushed up against him. I don't know... it just doesn't seem right to have this, like, download of Dagon dropped right into my brain. I crave privacy because I don't have much of it. Taking it away from someone else... no. I would never have done that on purpose.

Too bad I didn't have a choice.

I don't blame him for doing it, though. The essence exchange... it's a demon thing. When one of the Sombra demons finds their mate, they don't bother with the whole dating scene. If the gods picked out their mate for them, that's good enough, and to bypass the whole 'getting to know you' stage, their demon magic makes it so they can pass along everything about them with a touch of their hand.

Good thing it doesn't work that way for humans. It's bad enough he can use his other senses to tell what I'm thinking—and how horny I am for my demon. If he could get inside my head, see what it's really like to be Sierra Landry, he'd probably curse his gods for giving him such a flawed human to be his mate.

We all have flaws, demon or human. True, I refuse to delve too deep to find Dagon's since it wouldn't be fair, but there's a reason why I've spent nearly my whole life hiding behind the facade of my onstage alter ego.

Whiskey Rose is confident. Popular. Beloved.

Sierra... she's a jealous, insecure, paranoid mess.

Dagon said I was his one true mate. I don't know how much I was letting that influence me until right this very second when I realize that he has very vivid memories that feature another woman.

A *human* woman.

"No." The word is ragged, yanked from his chest. "Only you. You're the only one meant to touch me... to love me... to mate me. My body— it's yours. Always yours."

He's telling the truth. I don't know who that brunette woman that flashed into my brain is, but at the very least, she's never touched him. She's never seen him naked.

Only I have... and, suddenly, I feel a whole lot better about what I'm doing.

"So you're a virgin."

"Untouched, yes," he groans.

"I'm touching you now," I tease.

"Then unmated."

Right. A virgin.

I'm not about to fuck him. That would make things way too complicated, especially when he's convinced that I'm the one woman he's waited centuries to find and claim. But touching his cock might have helped him with his lust while only making mine *worse*.

An intimate touch, huh? You know what's more intimate than a hand job?

A blowjob.

He's close. The tension in his big body isn't only from the way I interrogated him between stroking him. His claws are digging into the magenta cushion we're sitting on—and, honestly, I don't give a shit. Couches can be replaced. Even antique settees can be replaced.

Going down on a five-hundred-year-old demon for the first time?

Now *that's* a unique experience...

I scoot back on the couch, bending my legs at my knees, kicking my feet into the air. I'm on my belly in the perfect position to angle his cock toward my lips.

I drop my head into his lap.

"Sierra? My mate? What are you doing?"

Isn't it obvious? "You just told me this body is mine, didn't you? Now lay back, demon, and let me suck my cock."

Gripping him by the base, I make a good effort. I really try. This is his first time. I want him to enjoy it, but no matter how I try to relax my jaw, I can't take much more than the head.

Dagon doesn't seem to mind. The moment my lips wrap around the head, my tongue swirling against his heated flesh, he murmurs my name again like it's a goddamn prayer.

Feeling bold—and probably just a touch delusional—I try to take some more, scraping him with the edge of my teeth.

I hit my limit quickly, gagging as I take too much. For a second, I struggle to breathe because genius Sierra seemed to have forgotten she had a fucking nose, but just as I'm about to give up and go back to stroking him, something... something happens.

He *changes.*

Dagon is still thicker than any human guy I've ever been with, but all of a sudden, I can suck a good three inches into my mouth, no problem. I hollow my cheeks, using suction to steal another moan from my demon, then release him with a slight *pop.*

I blink.

Okay... his dick is definitely different. It looks like him when he's that featureless mass of shadows, only there's no denying he has an inky black dick pointed up at me.

I glance up at *him*. To my shock, the rest of Dagon is the same as before: rust-colored skin, ridges over his nose, pointed ears, muscles for days. But his dick... that's pure shadow.

What?

How?

"When I'm in my shadows, I can control my size," Dagon explains. "It's the same for certain parts of my body. My cock. My hair. My claws... I can make them shadow without changing forms."

Well, that explains why he hasn't accidentally scratched me yet. If he made them shadow, he could stroke me with his fingers and never use his claws on me.

As for his cock...

"And you still feel my tongue on you like this?"

His gaze turns heavy-lidded as he exhales again. "I feel more pleasure in my shadows than I do when I'm demon."

I'll have to remember that.

For now, I take advantage of him changing his shape so that it's better suited for me. I wasn't exaggerating when I thought he was close before. All it takes is a few nibbles, a couple of pointed licks, and taking him as deep as possible, then sucking him again before my mouth is full of something hot, something salty, something... *smoky*?

Whatever it is, it's Dagon, and I swallow it gladly.

Once I lift my head from his lap, my demon reaches down to pat my head. As I wipe the corner of my mouth with the edge of my thumb, I try not to think about how the action is so similar to how I pet my cat.

"Thank you."

I rise up further that I'm resting on my knees. Patting his thigh in return, I tell him, "Don't mention it."

His hand lands lightly on the curve of my ass. "If that's what my mate wants, I won't mention the pleasure she's given me with her wicked tongue." Dagon sounds so solemn, I can't help but giggle—until he adds, "But I would like to use my tongue to taste her cunt now."

That's when I coo in surprise.

I didn't blow him because I expected him to reciprocate. But when he looks so eager as I meet his blazing red gaze, how can I say no?

Following my lead, he lays his palm possessively on my ass cheek. "May I? I've never done that before, either, but I will strive to give you as much pleasure as you gave me."

"I mean, if you *want* to—"

Wow, is he strong. All it takes is that one hand on

my ass for him to heft me up and lay me out on the settee.

So he told me that he can turn his claws to shadows. Right now? They're sharp as hell as he uses them to slice my poor legging into ribbons in his haste to get to my pussy.

Leggings... leggings can be replaced, too.

I sense his hunger. I sense his anticipation. It's not the mate sickness that's making him like this, either. This is Dagon finally getting to do something he's dreamed of for five fucking centuries.

And, yet, when I say, "Wait," he freezes in place before he can attempt to cut off my panties.

"My mate?"

Sorry, demon. It's one thing to blow him in the living room. If I'm going to teach my demon how I like my pussy licked, I want to be comfortable.

"In the bedroom," I tell him. I'm already panting softly, the anticipation of his hot mouth on my pussy making me almost crazed with lust. I hold out my arms. As though he knows exactly what I want, he swoops me up, shifting me so that I'm being carried bridal-style. "Take me there."

His eyes brighten. "And I can taste you in your quarters?"

I barely nod once before he's bounding out of the living room, toward the bedroom.

I do stop him one more time before I let him get

that first taste. I have plenty of leggings in my walk-in closet, but I happen to really like these panties. So, rather than let him slice them off, I shimmy out of them. Then, for good measure, I strip off my shirt and my bra.

I'm hot. Maybe I am sick after all because my whole body feels like it's on fire, but in a *good* way. Still, I'm a little sweaty, very horny, and I get a tiny bit of relief once I'm completely bare.

I expected him to immediately bury his face in my pussy. Honestly? If he wasn't distracted by his first glimpse of my naked body, he might have.

He's staring at me in wonder. For a split second, I think it's my tits that have his attention until I realize that the direction of his stare is a little lower than that.

"Dagon? You okay, demon?"

Reaching out, he trails his claw along my rose.

"This is beautiful."

It's the only tattoo I have. I got it to spite my mother, who had spent the first sixteen years of my life micromanaging every part of my appearance. I love it, but it hurt so fucking bad, I've never gotten another one.

"Thanks. I've always liked it." He's still staring at it, and that makes me wonder. "What's the matter? Don't you have body art in Sombra?"

He nods. "Yes. I've always envied the males who get to mark their chests." He smiles, showing off his fangs as he positions himself on the edge of the bed, right between where my legs are. "One day soon, I will cover mine for you."

"With roses?" I tease, nudging his nipple with my big toe.

"You are not Rose, my mate. That's what you told me. You are Sierra." He pulls his hand away from my side, taking my foot between his thick fingers instead. Slowly, carefully, he lowers it to the bed, then bats my instep lightly with the back of his hand. I know exactly what he wants, and I widen my legs as much as I can so that he can move closer to my pussy.

Those fangs of his might've made me a little apprehensive there for a moment, but it disappears a moment later as Dagon blows a warm breath out on my mound. I shiver at the sensation, and I see another smile tugging on his lips. It's a hungry one, echoed in his blazing eyes, and I've never been so amped to have a guy's mouth on me until right this very moment.

"You are *my* Sierra," he growls before dipping his face low enough to run the length of his tongue up my slit.

I've always wanted to be someone's Sierra. Even if it's only for tonight, I can be Dagon's.

After he gets his first taste, murmuring just how delicious it is, he nuzzles my clit with his nose as he uses his tongue to explore every bit of me down there. From my labia to actually breaching my entrance with the tip, what he lacks in experience, he more than makes up for with enthusiasm.

Dagon shifts his face to press kisses to my inner thigh before taking a deep breath and diving back in. I thread my fingers through his thick hair, pulling him closer, hoping he doesn't suffocate down there.

Immortal, I remind myself. I think it takes more than eating pussy to take out a fierce hunter like Dagon... and if that thought seems like it comes from him more than me, I ignore it because I'm careening toward coming the hardest I have in a long time.

And that's when I hear it.

"Knock, knock."

Shit.

Dagon's head whips up, turning toward the door. I already know how impressive his senses are, so I would've expected him to catch on to our intruder before they made it to my bedroom door.

I guess not if he has a nose full of pussy, and my taste on his tongue.

Fuck!

I start kicking a little, trying to get him away from me and out of the bed. Not because I *want* to, but because there's no way in hell I can let anyone catch us like this. I could care less about me—and considering who's out there, he'd probably just ask to join us if only to be able to brag he had a threesome with a *demon*— but Dagon...

That stupid first law thing. If anyone else sees him, he doesn't just get out of my hair. He gets thrown into demon *jail*.

And maybe I'm feeling a lot more magnanimous toward him after the way he was about to make me come harder than I have in ages, but I don't want to reward his enthusiasm by seeing him chained up and locked away in his world.

"Go," I snap, tapping him on the side with enough force to catch his attention. "Go before he walks in here and sees us."

Dagon doesn't say anything. He just furrows his brow and frowns, a hurt look twisting his features as the doorknob starts to turn.

For fuck's sake, this is like getting caught in a compromising position by my former manager all over again. After Jared cheated on me with Tandy, I thought I could get over my heartache by fucking one of the members of U R My Girl, Jared's rival boyband. I don't even remember which of the three blondies it was, only that he didn't have any idea what he was doing, and I was mortified when Cleo found him bouncing on top of me when I was supposed to be getting my hair done for a photoshoot.

Of course, what's his name—Brandon, that's right, it was *Brandon*—told everyone that we got caught because I was screaming his name loudly, not because I was late to an appointment. Cleo kept it under wraps so it was mostly industry gossip instead of being splashed over the tabloids, but she never let me forget how disappointed she was in me.

That was one of the reasons why I replaced her with Billie by the time I was twenty. Well, that and how Cleo was another one who was embezzling funds from me, but her being a judgey prude didn't help...

Jared Turner won't judge me for getting action where I can. But if he finds out demons are real?

That will *definitely* be blasted all over the news.

"Do you want to get dragged back to Sombra in chains?" I hiss.

"You are worried for me."

"Yes! Now disappear!"

Dagon nods, and just as the door starts to swing inward, the big demon vanishes into mist again.

CHAPTER 13
JARED TURNER

SIERRA

Out of everyone I know, Jared Turner is the only one who's never respected my 'closed door' rule.

Part of that is because he's self-centered. Since he's spent more than his fair share of evenings locked behind a closed door *with* me, it never would occur to him that my rule applies to him, too. The bigger, more obvious part is that he's too hyped up on his own fame and importance to care.

Doors are never closed to the superstar. He goes where he wants, when he wants, and his walking right into my bedroom as if he has any right to is no exception.

Dagon barely disappeared before we were caught.

So consumed with that, I didn't even think about the fact that I'm lying in bed, bare-assed naked. There's just enough time for me to slam my legs closed so that he doesn't see how fucking wet I am or how swollen my pussy is, but that's about all before Jared pops his head into my room.

Fifteen years after I met him and Jared Turner is as good-looking today as he was when I was sixteen. His blond hair has darkened, there are fine lines bracketing his pretty brown eyes that he hides beneath gobs of stage make-up, but that smile of his...

I used to do terrible things for that smile.

It widens as he gets a good look at me. "Ah, Rosie, babe. I hope you didn't get started without me."

I'm clearly naked. My nipples are hard as rocks, my hair is a mussed-up mess from where I writhed against the pillows, and I can only imagine how my face looks on the heels of nearly orgasming on my demon's face.

Because of his fucking awful timing, I'd gotten started with Dagon, but Jared interrupted before I could *finish*.

My gut twists from unfulfilled lust. The heat from Dagon's mouth only adds to the fire of my disappointment, and the sole target I have for that is striding into my room, already starting to remove his suit jacket.

I stop him before he undoes the first button in his shirt.

"What are you doing here?"

Jared pauses, his smile turning cocky. "You invited me."

"No, I didn't."

Yes, I did.

Shit.

Friday night seems like a lifetime ago; a lifetime before I met my demon. I can't believe it, but I completely forgot all about sending that text to Jared until he pulls his phone out of his pocket, showing me the screen.

"You asked if I was in town. I wasn't on Friday, but I made it back this afternoon. Figured I'd grab some food, freshen up, then visit my favorite girl."

Translation: I was working all weekend, I'm ready to fuck, and you're always ready for my dick.

Sorry about that, Jared. If you'd answered me on Friday instead of leaving me on read, maybe I could've told you any future tête-à-têtes between us were off. Because no matter what happens between my demon and me, I somehow have gotten enough respect for myself back that I'm not just going to let Jared fuck me and run.

Not when I've seen what it's like to be worshiped by a male who actually gives a shit about me...

I grab my blanket, covering up. That should've been a big clue that I wasn't interested in a quickie with Jared, but he grins before taking another step toward my bed.

I throw up my hand, warding him off. "Dude. Stop. I'm not fucking you."

Jared frowns. "Why not?"

That he asks at all just pisses me off more. "Because I don't want to? Isn't that enough of an answer for you? Because I said no?"

His expression turns wounded. A split second later, he grins again. "Oh. I get it. You're screwing with me, Rosie. I know you. You're not going to have me come all this way, be waiting in bed naked, then turn me away for whatever stupid reason you've suddenly come up with now that I've made time for you."

Stupid reason? "Goddamn, but you're an arrogant dickhead. You really think I spent two, three days waiting for you to grace me with your presence?"

He smirks. "Well, it's not like you'll invite anyone else to your bed."

I'm not a demon. My eyes don't glow like Dagon's.

Doesn't matter.

I'm seeing red all of a sudden anyway.

"Maybe you're right." And maybe my demon lover is hiding in the shadows, probably contemplating all of the ways he can eviscerate you. "And maybe I've finally decided to respect myself and my body a little more than just letting *you* have it."

"Oof. I think you've been spending too much time with your cats, babe. That was fierce." After miming slashing me with his blunt manicured fingernails—

nothing as intimidating... or sexy... as Dagon's claws—Jared raises his eyebrows at me, popping the first button on his shirt. "I like it."

In the corner, I hear a growl that has to be Dagon. Jared pauses for a moment, obviously dismissing the sound as belonging to Three, but I know that my ex is pushing my demon's limits.

I have to get him out of here. There's no time to call up security to drag him out, but I do have a foolproof method for making Jared Turner disappear.

"If you like me so much, why has it been a month since I've seen you?"

He freezes. That grin slides right off of his face as he groans in an over-the-top, theatrical way. "Seriously, Rosie? That's why you're turning me away? Because I've been busy? We can't all take a break when work gets tough."

You, asshole. I always knew Jared was one, but this isn't the first time he's easily dismissed the traumatic things in my life. After Patrick Ridgefield, Jared ghosted me for three months. Then, just when I was desperate enough to see him before I set out for the West Coast, California happened and, poof, he vanished.

Is that what he thinks I'm doing now? Taking a break because I don't want to be out on tour?

Considering what he says next, the answer is 'yes'.

He shakes his head slowly, like he's sorry for me. "I

know it has to be embarrassing. Your voice cracking like that while you're on stage? See... that's why I aways insist on a lip-syncing track. Saves my pipes, and let's be honest. Our fans don't come out to see us to hear perfect vocals." He gestures at me, then himself. "They want us, Rosie. Just us."

Yeah. I know. And while I will give my fans every part of me—including live vocals at each performance—Jared still doesn't seem to get what it's like when the obsession of one of them turns dark.

This isn't even about California.

This is about Ridgefield—and when I snap at him, we both know it.

"You never even reached out to me!"

"Of course I did." He shrugs. "I had my assistant call yours."

"You know damn well Billie isn't my assistant. And you've got my number." Obviously. "Texts go both ways."

"I was busy!"

I'm sure he was. "What's her name?"

He scoffs. "Jealous?"

My emotions are all over the place. To make it even worse, I got so wrapped up in the old drama with Jared, I forgot what I was doing—and who else is in the room. My demon is definitely jealous, and maybe that's spilling over to me, but I'm suddenly so envious I can't see straight.

But not of Jared. Fuck that. I haven't been jealous of this prick since I found out he was fucking Tandy behind my back. If she could take him so easily, she was welcome to have him.

It's not Tandy's red hair and sultry face that flashes in my mind's eye right now. It's that same human brunette I've seen before... the one that's straight out of Dagon's essence.

I shake my head, careful to keep the blanket up and over my boobs. "No!"

Jared chuckles. "You never could lie to me. But you don't have to be jealous. She's nothing. No one. She doesn't mean anything to me, Rosie. Not like you do."

Do you know how many times I've fallen for that? Billie probably does. In my own twisted way, I've spent half my life convinced that Jared Turner and I have a bond that transcends anything else. Sure, these days, it's all about sex. He would have no problem at all cheating on whatever poor woman he's seeing nowadays, so long as it's with me.

Suddenly, my jealousy turns to regret. As much as I've blamed him for cheating on me with Tandy, how many times have I *been* the Tandy for someone else?

I have a bond now. I'm not sure what's going to come of it, but it's just not sex that I'm cutting my ex off from tonight.

I'm done with him.

I'm done with this back and forth. I'm done with trying to explain.

I'm done with all of this.

I sigh. "I think you should go."

"Rosie—"

I've spent years trying to convince Jared to call me by my birth name. It never worked, and I gave up a long time ago.

Until now.

"My name is Sierra. And if you don't go, I'm gonna call Roy."

For all his blustering, if there's one person that Jared respects—though it's probably more of an intimidation thing—it's Roy. I hate to use Roy against him, but I'm... I'm done.

And his reaction tells me that he finally realizes that.

Screwing up his face in a nasty expression that the world never sees from the crooner, he snaps, "I made you. If it wasn't for me, you wouldn't have any of this."

He's right. I wrote "Heart Barely Used" because of him.

"But you broke me first." I shrug. "I think we're even, don't you?"

I don't have to resort to calling Roy. Jared storms out of my bedroom, and after I tug on a robe and follow after him, I make sure he gets on the elevator from my post on the opposite side of the living room. That was about as far as I could dare go away from Dagon without triggering the fire again, and I wait there until Jared's gone.

My phone was in my hand just in case I needed it. Once he's gone, I make a quick call down to the front desk, removing Jared Turner from the very small list of people who are allowed entrance directly into the apartment.

Dagon is still waiting in the bedroom. I can sense him in the corner, and when I narrow my gaze, searching, I see the faint outline of his mist.

I shudder out an exhale. "You can come back. He's gone."

Within seconds, my big demon is in front of me, fire in his eyes and a scowl on his face.

I'm immediately on guard. After putting up with Jared, I don't think I want to deal with Dagon's obvious jealousy next.

Especially when I'm struggling with my own.

Still, I'm not surprised when the first thing he says is, "That was him? Your former mate?"

I can't deny it, can I? "Yes—"

Dagon snarls. "He does not treat you like he is a former mate."

"Well, that's tough shit for him, then." And, true, maybe he wasn't really *former* when he walked in here since we've been friends with benefits for years... but he sure the hell is now. "And don't snarl at me. I told you that I've been with guys before. You didn't mind before. What changed?"

"He saw you bare!"

"And? Newsflash, Dagon: I've had sex with him before. I know you don't want to hear that, but it's true. He's seen me naked a lot. But, if it makes you feel any better, I didn't want him to see me naked now. I covered up. I didn't have to, but I did."

In response to mine, he reins in his anger. "I'm sorry. You're right. You're right about all of it. It's just... his lust for you was almost as potent as mine. I worried you would respond to it. That you still loved him."

"You could've asked me, you know. Instead of jumping down my throat."

Dagon's face goes blank. "I did not jump down your throat, my mate. You swallowed my cock in it, but you did so willingly."

Oh my God. "That's not what that means... you know what? Forget it."

And if he thinks we're going back to what we were doing before, he can forget that, too.

I storm away from Dagon. I don't know where I'm going, and I mutter in frustration when Three wakes up from his nap on the armchair just in time to notice how pissed I am. In a stunning sense of self-preservation, my cat yowls softly, hops off the chair, then scrabbles out the door before he can get caught in my path.

If Dagon was smart, he'd do the same.

Oh, wait. He can't. If he goes too far from me, he'll burst into flame.

Okay. If he was smart, he'd drop the subject. I'm not about to hop back into bed with him to distract him, but he should've learned enough about me by now to let it go.

And whether he did or not, he *doesn't*.

Instead, he lets out a roar of frustration so loud, if Three hadn't already bolted, that would've done the trick for him. He doesn't seem to mind Dagon's presence at all, but a roar? Even Three couldn't forgive that.

Me? I'm not even a little taken aback by it, and isn't that a change from just the other day?

I raise my eyebrow at him. "Yes? You have a problem?"

"Yes. I *do*."

SIERRA

O h.

"Then what is it? Come on, demon. Let's get it all out in the open."

He points a claw at me. "See? That's it right there. The problem is that we shouldn't have to do that. You are my mate. If I had your essence, I would know exactly how I failed you and what I should do to fix it." Another, softer roar escapes him. "This is the most frustrating hunt. I make the wrong steps because, with you, Sierra, I am hunting without all of my senses."

Normally, a comment like that would earn a flippant response. And I have one right on the tip of my tongue before I have to admit something: he's right. He's used to doing things the Sombra way. All the other demons get their mate's essence so they know how best to 'woo' them.

I got Dagon's, and I used it to keep him at arms-length as long as possible. So I only made it a couple of days. I did what I could.

And he's let me. He's in a whole new world, trying his best to prove himself, and I've made it difficult for him for no reason other than my own hang-ups.

I was keeping it to myself. Honestly, I don't even think I did so consciously. It's just... I've spent so much of my life being Whiskey Rose. I've kept Sierra for me, and even though I let him call me that, I never let him in.

I didn't think it was fair that I could read him, but he couldn't read me. My solution was to try to block him off as much as possible.

That obviously didn't work.

Maybe... maybe it's time I let him in just a little.

Before I can second-guess what I'm about to do, I march over to Dagon. Then, wrapping my fingers around his forearm, I open myself up as much as I can. I don't know if this is working, but I imagine myself sharing everything with him that I've kept hidden, even from Billie.

Dagon jolts, and when his eyes flare so brightly, they're almost blinding, I think I did it.

He dips his head, locking eyes with me. I squint, and seeing so, he turns the blinders off. His face is wearing an awed expression, and with his eyes merely glowing at their normal rate, I can't miss it.

"You *desire* me."

Ah, crap.

Welp, thanks, essence. Even if I thought I was getting away with pretending like I haven't been eager to sleep with Dagon since I first realized it was possible, with the essence exchange, he knows everything about me.

And he's marveling over the fact that I do want him.

Doesn't mean I can have him, though, and because I'm sure he can tell that from my essence, I keep quiet.

He takes a moment, and then, sounding even more stunned, he rumbles, "And you are jealous."

Fuck. Couldn't hide that, either, could I?

"You have no reason to be jealous, my mate. None at all."

"Yeah?" I shouldn't do it. I shouldn't throw it in his face...but then I do. "Who is the brunette from your memories then? The human?"

I was so shocked at first by his appearance. But Dagon... he never seemed to be put off by my being human. If he was only used to demoness women, wouldn't I look small? Scrawny? His ears are pointed, mine are round. I don't have horns, either, and my skin is a pale shade of brown while his is *red*.

But he never seemed surprised by what I looked like.

Because of her?

I don't know who she is, though she's popped into my head more than once. And I realize at that very moment that I've fallen harder for my demon than I ever should've because, all along, I've avoided digging too deep to protect myself.

Who was she? Another love, but one he couldn't have because she wasn't his *fated* mate?

Does he regret being paired up with me? Am I a replacement?

Will someone ever want *Sierra*?

Dagon's features screw up. "You're asking after Susanna?"

He feels such warmth when he says her name, I almost choke on my sudden envy. It's even worse that it's similar enough to *mine*.

Yup. I'm definitely jealous. "Forget it. I don't want to know—"

Before I can move out of his reach, Dagon swallows me up in his arms. "She is the duke's mate. You have no reason to be jealous of her. I think fondly of her because I've guarded her for decades... but she is not my mate. She is not *you*, Sierra."

I want so badly to believe him. Everything about Dagon tells me it's the truth, but it seems so impossible and... fuck it.

I melt into his arms, wrapping mine around his waist.

Dagon braces me with his broad hands clutching me through my robe. "Let me have you. Let me show you that you're the only female I've ever wanted. That I will ever desire as well."

I'm not surprised he's propositioning me. Considering what we were doing before—and the massive erection that's digging into my upper belly in this position—I would've been more surprised if he didn't.

I pull back. "You're only saying that because of the mate sickness—"

"I would've mated you the moment you summoned me to your quarters, Sierra. Claiming you... making you mine? That's never been a question for me. I want you madly. Desperately. I'll do anything for you. If you refuse me, I will wait. I will beg at your feet like your creature does for treats. I will take any scrap you throw my way."

The earnestness chokes me up even more than the jealousy did. "Dagon..."

"Let me taste you. Let me kiss you. Let me love you... let me have you any way I can because I am already yours."

Honestly?

I've been talked into doing worse by someone who didn't mean half of the flowery words he said. Jared had fifteen years to learn how to keep me dangling on his hook, even though he never realized I had him wrapped around my finger, too.

Dagon? He knows just how to sweet talk me in *days.*

I can't even blame it on the essence, either. I was more than eager to shove his face between my legs when I still had mine, riding high only on having his.

Now we've shared it. He knows me, he knows how much I want him... and, still, he's giving me complete control over what happens between us next.

And he's right. I *do* desire him. I've been fantasizing about him for days, and though I tried to ignore it, I'm still worked up from him bringing me to the brink of completion before.

I take a deep breath, realize that this was always inevitable once I stopped being afraid of him, and shrug my robe off of my shoulders.

Dagon groans as my boobs are revealed to him again. "Sierra..."

I step back, making it so that I can remove the rest of the fabric.

Once naked, I give him a daring grin. "You want to take me? Alright, demon. Go right ahead."

He only hesitates a moment. I'd bet my stake in the Dorado that he was checking my essence, making sure that I one hundred percent meant it when I told him he could have me. And since I do... I let out a squeal of delight when he swoops me up, tossing me gently over his broad shoulder before stalking over to the bed.

It's so easy to forget what happened between us the last time he laid me out on the bed and when he's doing it now. At least, for me, it is. As though Dagon wants to be sure that he can finally have a chance to fuck me before we get interrupted again, he lays me out, then marches back over to the door.

He makes sure it's closed, then is back at the foot of the bed before I know it. One knee climbs up on the mattress, his weight creating a slight dip that I fall into.

Another knee and he's caged in my legs. From my position, all I see is the hungry look on his face as he looms over me, and his dick coming for me.

I swallow, a hint of nerves creeping in.

Dagon immediately responds to it. Right before my eyes, he turns his cock to shadow again; he does the same to his claws. Changing the shape and size like he did when I went down on him, he suddenly looks a lot more manageable.

And I'm suddenly very eager to find out what that'll feel like inside my pussy.

"Are you prepared for me to claim you, my mate?" Dagon rumbles.

"*Yes.*"

He takes each of my ankles in his hands, easing my legs open like he did before. He urges me to wrap my legs around his waist before he scoots forward, bracing his hands on each side of my shoulders.

I fist the sheets in mine, waiting for him to take control.

It's his turn now—and I *need* it almost as much as I need him.

Dagon knows that, too. His cock nudges at the entrance of my pussy, but I'm too slick, too wet for him to lodge himself inside. Before I can give him a hand, he shifts his hip, releasing one hand to grip the base of his cock. He lines us up himself, then pushes just enough that I take the first two inches easily.

I close my eyes and moan.

"How is that, my mate?"

"It's perfect," I promise.

"I can make myself smaller so that it fits easier."

And get rid of the delicious way I'm feeling stuffed right now? I kick him in his taut ass cheek. "Leave it. You were right. We'll fit. Watch." I lift my hips off of the bed, taking even more of him. "See?"

Dagon shudders out a breath. "Your cunt is hugging my cock."

I'm sure it is. "Now move, and see how good that feels. I promise. It's even *better*."

I love how implicitly Dagon trusts me. He did before he had my essence, and now? As though dipping into my past, seeing how I've been fucked before, how I *like* it, he proceeds to do just that.

I don't even have to do anything. Despite never being a pillow princess before, with my virgin demon, I figure it's worth it. I don't know what he likes because *he* doesn't know yet. I want him to explore, whether it's taking one of my boobs in his hand, lapping at it with his heated tongue, or lifting my leg high so he can get a better angle as his thrusts deepen, I do exactly what he asked of me.

I let him take me.

Because of how close I was before, I come almost immediately. I just needed the penetration and a little stimulation before I'm squeezing his dick, gasping his name as I climax. The moment I do, that really turns my demon on. His thrusts become more forceful, his hold on me even more possessive... just how I like it.

But because this is his first time, I knew he wouldn't last long. He lasts longer than I guessed he would, and when his thrusts become jerky, his breathing heavy, I expect him to finish any moment now.

And that's when he starts murmuring to me.

"My heart is in your hands."

For some reason, everything in me is singing for me to echo that back to him—so I do. "My heart is in your hands."

"Our lives will be forever intertwined."

I feel like they have already. "Our lives will be forever intertwined," I admit.

"I give myself to you." Dagon pauses, thrusting so deeply into me, I'm not sure where I end or he begins. "I give you *everything*."

"I do, too," I swear. "I give myself to you. I give you everything, my demon."

The moment I finish that last sentence, Dagon roars for a final time. It's my name, and he shouts it right as he shoots his load inside of me before collapsing just to my side.

We're still connected, but he's careful not to crush me with his big demon body. I'd appreciate that, too, if something really weird wasn't going on.

It's over almost as quickly as it began, and though me moving as fast as I do to sit up has Dagon's cock slipping out of me, I couldn't care less at the moment.

"What the fuck was that?"

Dagon's eyes have dimmed to the point they look like flickering flames. I can still see the satisfied look on his face, though, as he murmurs, "That's exactly what that was, my love."

My love?

I shake my head, rubbing my boobs. "Not funny, demon. Something just happened. Something inside of my chest. It's like it—"

"Snapped into place?"

"Yes."

"That was our bond. It's finalized now."

It *what*?

I scoot away from him before climbing out of the bed. "Did you know that would happen?"

Dagon is frowning now. "That we would be bonded when you gave me the mate's promise as I claimed you? Of course. You have my essence. You knew that, too."

Um, no. I didn't.

Wait—

Promise?

My eyes go wide. "Is that what you had me say? That was a *promise*?"

He nods. "It was your vow to me. I made it to you, too. That's why we're bonded."

And there's no breaking a bond.

Are you kidding?

I... I...

I don't know what to say.

Dagon can tell that I'm on the edge of losing it again. Sliding across the bed, he turns toward me. He bows his body just enough not to look intimidating, keeping his voice soft.

"Sierra? Talk to me. Tell me what you're thinking."

Really? "What? My *essence* isn't telling you?"

The big demon flinches. For a split second, I feel guilty about that. It's the essence that's gotten me into trouble. I gave him mine and he immediately used it. Of course he thought I've been digging into his all along.

Of course he thought I knew what I was doing.

But I didn't, and though I know I shouldn't take that out on him... he's the only one here.

"How dare you!"

"Sierra. I've upset you—"

"No shit."

His frown deepens. "I don't know what I did wrong, but I will make it better. Retrieve your creature. I will conjure the portal back to Sombra, and once the three of us are in my lair, I will do anything to make you smile."

That is quite possibly the worst thing he could've said to me.

"Get Three? You think me and my cat are going with you to your demon world?"

"Of course—"

Oh, hell no. "Okay, Dagon. You want me to tell you what I'm thinking? Fine. You can conjure a portal back to your demon world all you want. That's your business. I'm not going with you. Neither is Three."

"You are my mate—"

Yeah. I've heard that one before. "And?"

Dagon firms his jaw. "I am returning to Sombra. I must."

My stomach twists. Dagon appeared in my life two fucking days ago. *Two*. And maybe it's because most people I meet are here and gone again, measuring our relationship in minutes and empty conversations before we part ways forever, but those two full days with Dagon meant something to me even if I fooled myself into thinking this would only last the weekend.

This is his fault for expecting too much from me, but it's mine, too. I wanted a weekend of fun. He made it clear from the beginning he believed I was the one female he spent centuries waiting for, and while I didn't *mean* to lead him on... I think I did.

Worse, I recklessly gave him something I don't have the ability to promise: *forever.*

That's what happened. The certainty is so clear, I'm not sure if it's coming from Dagon or from me. When I initiated sex with him, so turned on by the jealous way he reacted to Jared... I wasn't thinking about what came next.

I sure as fuck wasn't thinking about what that promise I made meant when he had his big body braced over mine, his dick stretching me out, that look of absolute adoration turning his harsh features *breathtaking...*

Dagon is sweet. He's kind. He has an innocence about him that comes from living a life so different from mine.

He's also growly. Possessive. Hard-headed. I didn't bother trying to explain that this could only be a weekend thing because he was so sure that we were endgame, and part of me must've fallen prey to his essence inside of me because I... I wish we could be.

Maybe, if he wanted to stay here, we could have made it work. When it comes to a relationship, I need two things: loyalty and discretion. At this part of my career, it's essential. Baby Sierra never got over her heart being broken by her first love cheating on her. Sure, I own it now by having kept Jared Turner wrapped around my finger for so long. Knowing him, my sending him away while I was naked, he was horny, and he didn't get laid will have him being nasty at first before he starts doing anything he can for another chance.

It's the game we've played for more than a decade —but I'm done with that. I think I have been for a while.

As for discretion... that one is obvious.

With Dagon, he meets my two main requirements, and with a body like that to boot.

But I can't leave everything I've ever known to follow him to another world...

"You can go. I'm not stopping you." I couldn't if I tried. "But I'm staying here."

DAGON

I am confused.

The essence exchange was supposed to help me learn the true nature of my mate in an instant. And while I accepted Sierra's when she graciously offered it to me, that only makes it harder for me to understand her refusal to leave the human world.

She belongs with her mate. She belongs with *me*. And I? I have always planned on returning to Sombra as soon as I could open the pathway from her world back to mine. As my mate, she would come with me.

Sierra has had my essence from the moment we met. Surely she understood my intentions. All she would've had to do was search my existence and know that her male is a respected hunter in Caol. Of course I would bring her home to the village I've missed these last few decades.

We would have a lair together where we can build our family. I have her essence now. Though we haven't discussed it yet, Sierra is interested in having spawn one day. She loves her creature as if he were her kin—the same as she thinks of the other female who lives in her quarters—but she wants a babe of her own.

I can do that. On the next gold moon, should she wish it, I can give her my seed, and we can start that family... in Sombra.

So why, when she says that she has no intention of leaving her human city, does she unequivocally mean it?

I sense her determination like a blast from her side of the bond to mine. Though I don't understand why, she is certain she will stay here, with or without her male.

You can go. I'm not stopping you. But I'm staying here...

My heart stutters in my chest. I want to roar out in pain, though I don't if only because I'd rather ache than ever see my mate frightened of me again. Still, Sierra's cutting rejection wounds me worse than even the arkoda's claws.

Doesn't she understand? We are mates. I will forever be her shadow. We must be together, no matter what.

I must make her see. Though I'm looming, I try to

scale my shadows even as I reach out, picking up a stray lock of her hair with my claw. It's escaped the rope during our mating, messy and gorgeous and *mine.*

Just like this female.

The lock runs over my claw, fluttering back to her shoulder. The rest of my mate is covered with the fabric she stole from her bedding. That's for the best. I would only be distracted by her breasts and her cunt if she left herself uncovered.

This is my forever. I cannot allow myself to be distracted, not when so much is at stake.

"Sierra." She doesn't flinch at my rumble, or draw away when I stroke her soft hair again. I am emboldened and rub the side of my claw against her jaw, preening when she sighs, leaning into my touch. "I will not go anywhere without you."

Her eyes were partially closed. At my vow, they widen. "Are you... does that mean you're going to stay here?"

Follow in the paths of the other demons and stay in the human world? All I've seen of it has come from my glimpses out of Sierra's windows. Even through the walls of her quarters, it smells of oil and dirt, humans and waste. It's bright out, even when the shadows fall. It's noisy. For a hunter who is used to the oppressive silence of the shadows at the edge of Sombra, it's *deafening.*

I do not belong here. I belong with Sierra, but this world isn't mine.

"No," I tell her. "I must return to Sombra."

My debt to Susanna has been repaid. I promised I would serve her as her personal guard until the time I saved her life, or until I found my mate and gave her everything I have. I am an honorable demon. I've done what I vowed, and now it is time for me to return to Caol, return to the hunt, and devote the rest of my existence to proving to my mate that there is no male better than I for her.

That is all I want to do, and still Sierra refuses me.

She steps away from me. It's another rejection, and I whimper as I resist the urge to creep after her.

Her forehead creases at the sound. "Dagon…"

I straighten myself to my full height. A hunter can be vulnerable, but I want Sierra to be proud of me—so I must be proud myself. "I claimed you," I remind her.

That was a mistake. The hint of affection slipping down our band vanishes in an instant. So does the soft edge to her voice that was there when she murmured my name before.

Instead, she glowers up at me. "Look. It's been fun. I wanted a distraction from my life, and you've been the perfect one. But you need to stop with this 'claiming' BS. I want a partner, Dagon, not an owner."

I recoil in horror. "I do not want to *own* you. Not like that."

"Don't you? Don't you want to possess me?"

I want her to always be mine. That's what a true mate is. Not a master, but the other half of her. The male who will love her, protect her, and, yes, possess her... but only because she owns me and my heart.

And I struggle with explaining that to Sierra. She has my essence. She should *know*.

I am an honorable male, but not a patient one, and my frustration boils over as I imagine Sierra easily walking away from me, knowing that I am destined to forever follow her.

She should want me to stand at her back—and she doesn't.

Where did I go wrong?

"You are my mate—"

She stomps her tiny foot on the floor. "You don't get it, do you? I can't be your mate!"

My shadows drift away in the force of her explosion.

I have angered her. Worse, my confusion doubles when I realize I don't know what it is she is saying to me? It's Sombran, and yet I still do not understand. "Sierra..."

She makes a soft sound, losing her sudden fury. "I'm Whiskey Rose. Being with you... I forgot that for a minute. But I can't. And I know it's a fucking cliche, but it's not you. Okay? It's me. I have to stay here. You could, too, if you wanted to. I'm sure we can find a way to make this work—"

"I love you, my mate." It shouldn't be such a surprise for her to hear that, but I think it is. I repeat myself. "I love you, Sierra. But I am Sombran—"

"Yeah. You love me, but not enough to give up something important. And I get it. Trust me, I get it. Because, for fuck's sake, I *am* Whiskey Rose. I have responsibilities. I have fans. Contracts. You think you claimed me? Well, get in line, Dagon. The public got their claws in me first."

Her bitterness burns, but though she's addressing me, I get the sense that her ire isn't truly meant for me.

And then, before I can try to soothe my mate, she juts out her chin. "You can create a portal now, right? I bet that means you can leave me without going up in flames. So why don't you do me a favor and sleep in the guest room? Unless you just want to get our goodbyes over with and head on home yourself."

I open my mouth, but no words come out. My mate... she is sending me away? Not out of her quarters entirely unless I choose to go, but certainly her personal sleeping area?

That doesn't make sense. This... this is all wrong.

There is no denying that she is my one true mate. The gods gave her to me. My mate summoned me, then gave me her body. She took my seed. She repeated the mate's promise in the moments before I

released inside of her cunt. We've finalized our bond…
so why is she sending me away from her now at all?

The gods have a queer sense of humor. Our new
bond will allow us to have distance between us. I won't
burn away to my shadows if she goes too far from me,
but that's only because we're tethered together for the
rest of our immortal lives. No matter where she goes, I
can find her.

I can chase her.

If I must, I can hunt my mate and return her to my
side…

The spare sleeping area is not that far from where
Sierra slumbers. If she needs space from me to process
my essence and her emotions, the least I can do is offer
that to her.

I nod solemnly. This is wrong—but the blame is on
my shoulders.

I will fix this. No matter what it takes, I will, and
that begins with respecting her enough to do as she
asks.

"I will not go to Sombra without you—"

Under her breath, I hear her mutter, "So fucking
stubborn."

I am. I am also *hers*. "I will not take a portal, but I
will go to the spare sleeping area if you wish it, my
mate."

"Uh. Yeah. I'm sorry, Dagon, but right now? I think
that's for the best."

Maybe it is.

She bites down on her bottom lip. "Do you need me to remind you where it is?"

I shake my head. "I have your essence now. I will find it."

Her pale cheeks develop a lovely pink color. "Right. I forgot. So you know everything about me now."

I do, which is how I can admit that, once Sierra makes up her mind, there is very little that can be done to change it.

I also sense how uncomfortable that thought suddenly makes her. Because I've already upset her enough, I don't mention it. Instead, I run my gaze over her one last time for the evening, taking her in before I nod again, turning away from her.

As I force myself to walk out of her personal quarters, something fuzzy whispers against my shadows. Glancing down, I see Sierra's creature trotting alongside me at my feet.

Behind me, she mutters again, this time addressing Three. "Traitor. I'll remember that when you want wet food in the morning."

Does the creature understand her? Ungez are simple beasts, but Sierra's Three seems quite intelligent, although he does not speak.

I lower myself into a crouch so I can stroke my claws through his fur. "I am sorry for trying to hunt you. You are a good creature. Please, go back to Sierra. She needs you."

The furry creature twitches his ears. After bumping against my shadows one more time, finding the flesh past the edges as I feel his through his fur, Three yowls softly before turning around and trotting back through the open door.

Sierra's voice filters out of it. "Ah ha. Looks like you remembered who's responsible for the treat budget, huh?"

I smile, though another pang lances directly into my heart. I want so desperately to follow behind Three, hoping that my mate will have a tease for me. We only mated once. I have much more seed to offer her, but she won't welcome me now.

And all because I was too stubborn to think about what it is my mate desires...

⁂

THE SPARE ROOM IS COLD AND EMPTY WITHOUT SIERRA'S light. Her scent faintly overlays the space, making it easier for me to be separated from my mate so soon after bonding her to me, but it's not enough. Her sweat and musk on my skin keeps me sane, and though I'd give anything for her to welcome me again, I sit on the edge of the elevated nest in this room and dwell over where precisely I went wrong.

So determined to return to Sombra as soon as possible, I forgot what it meant to be a Sombra male. The essence exchange does more than allow a mate who is Other to communicate with her demon. It gives me an insight into my female. So while I disregarded it as I faced off against Sierra earlier, I rely on it now.

It all starts with one word: *responsibility.*

I've learned much of who my Sierra is in the time we've spent together; without her essence, it was essential that I did so myself. She told me of her 'movies', even honored me with her sounds—her songs—and confessed that she, too, had a rule similar to the duke's first law that she must follow.

I didn't understand that then. Now, Sierra's experiences flashing through my mind like another 'movie' with her as the star, I finally do.

She asked me once if there was someone in Sombra who everyone knew. In her world, Sierra is like Duke Haures. No matter where she goes, she is recognized, adored... even *hunted.*

There are those who want her for themselves. Even before she knew she was meant for a demon male, humans—including the one who walked in on our mating—tried to claim her. Some even promised to hurt her if they could not.

She is frightened. Not of me; at least, not once she understood instinctively that I would never harm her. She is frightened of those males who have no respect for her and her wishes, who'd rather see her gone than out of their reach.

You would think that, as her mate, I would know better.

I did not—and I was wrong. So determined to impress upon her my desires, I was no better than the human males who hurt her. I didn't listen. I didn't understand how important it was to her to perform her craft.

I do now.

I only hope that I have not broken our new mating beyond repair...

Our bond is solid. Across her quarters, I can *feel* Sierra. Her emotions slam into me, switching so swiftly, I get anger and hurt, pride and sorrow, regret and...

Lust.

I shudder, my cock stirring again.

Batting it with the back of my hand, I ignore my own desire. She feels lust, but her essence tells me that that is not uncommon for my feisty little mate. Though I'd rather not delve too deeply when it comes to her experiences with other males, I understand that my Sierra is not a demoness. Humans don't have one true mate. They can have as many as they choose, cramming in multiple matings in the single century they're given.

Until now. She has chosen me and will have no

other; our bond will make it so. But that doesn't mean that the lust she feels now is for me... and then, as clearly as if she were in front of me and not across her quarters, I hear my mate whisper my name.

"Dagon..."

My mate needs me, and though she banished me to this other room, nothing will stop me from going to her now.

CHAPTER 16
RAIN

SIERRA

It takes every bit of strength I have not to chase after Dagon.

I didn't think he would really go, and that just goes to show me that—once again—I don't know my demon at all. He never does anything I expect, and even when he does, it's so different than any other guy I've ever known.

And, fuck, that would be so refreshing if it wasn't for his sudden insistence that I follow him to his realm.

I thought he was kidding. The first time he mentioned bringing me home with him, I thought it was, like, for a trip. A way for him to show off his world.

Staying with him? Leaving Whiskey Rose behind?

It never even occurred to me that he was serious because, no matter how often I dreamed of giving it all up, of retiring, of enjoying the wealth I hoarded and finding some semblance of a *normal* life... it just never seemed possible.

Until Dagon seemed so sure I would hop right into a portal with him now, blow off the rest of my tour, and disappear without a word to my fans—or my found family.

What makes it worse? Is that I almost said 'yes'.

'Cause, look, being normal is vastly overrated. Not only that, but I seem to have acquired my very own shadow demon. How can things ever be normal again after that?

But leave Billie? Leave New York? Disappoint my fans?

I can't do that, even if some part of me desperately wants to.

So I lash out at Dagon instead. I know I'm doing it, but that doesn't stop me. And, hey, he has my essence now. He should be able to tell that I'm torn between what I should want and what I *do* want, and though going to Sombra with him is totally off the table for the moment, I don't actually want him walking away from me right now.

I know where he's going. Even if I didn't kick him out of my room and send him to the empty guest room, I *feel* him walking away from me. That tie—that bond

—that snapped into place between us after he nutted inside of me is like a goddamn *rope* tying us together.

Can you believe this? Some women get reckless, have unprotected sex, and get stuck with a baby or an STI. Me? I gave in to my lust and feelings for Dagon and I got—

Immortality.

Forever.

Dagon...

I get an impressive demon mate who thinks that, just because I let him fuck me, he gets to *claim* me.

The look on his face when I rejected him... he couldn't understand why this was only supposed to be a weekend full of distraction; why it *had* to be. Come Monday afternoon, Billie will be back. She lives here. How can I expect to keep any other humans from finding out about him when I have a roommate?

What about when I finally get cleared by my doctors and have to go back to being Whiskey Rose? I'm in the spotlight constantly. How can I expect my demon to love me from the shadows?

How can he expect me to sacrifice everything I've worked for my entire life to join him in another realm?

That's the gist of it. The problem right there. I've proven over the years that I can have discreet relation-ships so long as my partners keep their mouths shut and don't go running to the press. It's why I've kept Jared on the hook, using my ex at the same time as he's using me. For sex. For companionship. We both know how hard it is to date at our level of fame. I've basically given up on it at this point of my career while Jared... he's a grown man. I never twisted his arm to be with me, whether during our relationship or after. Like most things in my life, he's a distraction.

That's all Dagon was supposed to be. The spellbook, too. I read the spell because I was curious, not because I really believed there was such a thing as true love.

I've been around the block before. True love was for romance novels and chick flicks... so why am I so conflicted?

I want him. I want to keep him. Not like he's another Three, or a personal pet or anything. He's Dagon, and he swears he's mine, and I was getting kind of used to the idea—until I discovered that sleeping with him once means that we're it. There's no going back. There's no changing our minds.

We're mates, and I'm not sure how I feel about that.

If I were a normal woman who didn't have the world's eyes on her, maybe this would be a no-brainer. I've already hit my thirties, and if I want to have kids someday, I need to get a move on. Fooling around with Jared was fun, but I'd be lying if I said I didn't want *more.*

I wanted someone to love me. I wasn't picky about *who* so long as it was me they wanted, and not

Whiskey. But since there's never been a way to tell what motives another person truly has, I gave up on looking for my HEA years ago.

Dagon is so different, it really is fucking refreshing. Thanks to the essence exchange, I do know how he feels. What he's after.

Me.

He wants *me*.

He wants his mate, and it would be so, so easy to let him have her.

If I was a normal woman... but I'm not.

Fuck. I need another distraction. And since I booted him from my bed, that can't be Dagon. Heading out to the living room to watch a movie is out, and though we haven't had any dinner yet, my stomach is too twisted into knots to even think about eating.

I root around for my phone. Last time I remember seeing it, it was on my nightstand. I'd been ignoring it, enjoying my afternoon with Dagon, and after I kicked Jared out, too, I purposely refused to check it. Knowing him, when he works himself up over my rejection, I'll hear about it.

To my surprise, he hasn't started yet. I do, however, have a message that came through in the last twenty minutes.

It's from Billie.

> Rest of the weekend's off, S. I'm coming home.

Huh. That doesn't sound so good.

> Everything okay?

When the three little dots appear, I wait to see what Billie's response is—and it's almost exactly what I expected from her.

> It's fine.

> But we'll talk when I get home. I'm still in Connecticut now, but I should be leaving soon. Just gotta take care of something first.

> K… see you then.

I wait a few moments to see if she's going to answer again. When she doesn't, I bite down on my bottom lip, wondering what could have happened that would chase Billie back to New York this late.

She'll tell me. I might have the world's biggest secret that I've been keeping from her, but my best friend doesn't hide anything from me. She's the only person I know for sure never has, and whatever went down, I'll be here for her.

Too bad I'm still not distracted—and remembering

my secret has my mind turning right back to Dagon and how ready I was to spend the rest of the night banging his brains out before I realized what it cost me to sleep with him...

Ah, screw this.

I'm going to take a shower.

AH, YES. THIS IS JUST WHAT I NEEDED. AN ICY COLD shower to knock out the last of my lust.

The shock of the spray had me dragging my mind right out of the gutter. Kind of hard to continue fantasizing about Dagon's big body sprawled out over mine when the cold water is quickly erasing the last of his heat from my skin.

Once it does, I jerk the knob just enough so that the water temp is tolerable, then busy myself with scrubbing my scalp and shampooing the full length of my hair. That done, I condition it carefully before rinsing out all of the cream.

Ten minutes into pampering myself in the shower stall, though, I make a mistake. Using a washcloth to lather body wash all over my skin, a jolt of pleasure skitters down my spine when I trail the cloth over my nipple.

Damn it. I'm still feeling sensitive. It's even worse when I dip the cloth between my legs, my clit crying out for some more stimulation. And instead of rubbing the nub myself, all I can think about is Dagon between my legs, worshiping my pussy.

"Dagon..."

Shit. His name just slips out as I moan, wishing it was his tongue on my skin and not the damp washcloth.

Know what? I think I turned the shower from cold to warm too soon. This isn't as bad as the lust I was feeling this morning when he explained the mate sickness to me; in a way, it's *worse* because my body knows what sex with my demon is like.

And it craves it.

No. Down, girl. Going to Dagon right now would just be sending mixed signals—

—but what if *he* comes to *me*?

Because that's exactly what happens. Even as I can't resist reaching between my legs again, shocked by how slick and wet I am, I nearly slip and fall and land in a pile on the shower tile when, suddenly, the stall door flings outward.

And there he is. Eyes burning through the slight steam that might be coming from *me*, he's big and beautiful in his solid demon form, watching me as though seeing me wet and horny is all he's ever wanted in his long existence.

I don't bother covering myself up. After what we've spent most of the day doing... what's the point?

I do, however, snap at him. "Dagon? What are you doing in my bathroom?"

"You need me. You called to me down our bond, your body in need of mine. I am your male." His hand drops down to his naked groin—and the erection he's sporting. "I will always be here for you when you need me."

"What? No! I'm just taking a shower—"

"You are washing yourself clean of me, my mate. Using your indoor rain."

Indoor rain? Ah. The shower spray. "I'm just washing up. Us humans do that sometimes after sex. It's not a big deal."

"To a human male, perhaps. To a demon? I prefer it when our scents mingle. I prefer it when I smell of *you*."

I toss him the bottle of body wash. "Then use this."

Dagon catches it easily. He looks confused for a moment, but a few seconds later, he nods. "Your soap. Thank you, my mate. I shall."

And then the big demon steps into the shower stall with me.

"Dagon," I squeal, moving closer to the wall so that he can fit in here with me. "What are you doing now?"

"You offered your soap to me. I accepted your invitation to join you in your rain."

That was my mistake. I was being bitchy, and my demon is giving me more credit than I deserve. That, or it's another one of those slight miscommunications.

Whatever.

"I'm almost done anyway. I just have to finish rinsing off, then you can have the shower to yourself."

"I'd rather stay with you, my mate."

I'm sure he would. "Yeah, but I'm clean—"

"And, yet, I can still scent your cunt. No amount of soap can cover up your musk." Moving into me, Dagon presses his slick chest against my back, his big body just about caging me on this side of the stall. His hands land on my naked waist, keeping me right with him as his cock nestles itself between my ass cheeks. "I told you, Sierra. You need me."

He's right.

Fuck. I know I shouldn't. It's barely been a couple of days since I met Dagon and already I'm addicted to him. If he thrusts a little, positioning himself right at my entrance and gives a small push, I won't stop him.

So, instead, I demand with more than a hint of heat: "Is that it? You're going to use my attraction to you and sex to control me?"

I'd hate him if he did. It would work... but I would hate him.

I should've known better. He's as addicted to me as I am to him—thank you, mate bond—but he already showed me that he'd rather suffer blue balls than ever force me.

Shit. I was the one who had to convince *him* to let me go down on him. And it wasn't like my first time with Jared, how I knew I was going to let him bang me at least, but I wanted him to 'convince' me I should let him first. My demon really needed to know for sure that I was touching him because I wanted to, not because I felt pity for him.

A strange attraction to each other has never been a problem for us. Even when I came face to face with his demon shape and screamed, it wasn't long before I really took him in and realized that we were alike enough that I *could* fuck him once his essence assured me that—while he wanted to fuck me, too—he would never do it against my will.

That's not how Sombra demon males are wired. I'm the only woman—the only female—he'll ever have because I am his gods-given mate... and he waited five hundred years for me.

If I shove him out of the shower right now, he'll go. No doubt about that. Even though we're bonded now, he won't just take me—and he reinforces that with his answer.

"Never." His breath is so warm on the back of my neck that the spray from the shower seems even icier in comparison. He nuzzles the wet skin of my shoulder with the point of his chin. "Your cunt is a gift, my mate. I will only ever take it when you offer it to your male."

For him to reach my shoulder with his chin while

the blunt head of his cock prods the side of my pussy, he has to have his big body bowed over mine. I glance down, looking just past my hip. Dagon has his legs braced and bent, hands placed possessively on my waist. With the right angle, I could totally give him complete access to the rest of my body.

He hopes I will. He's desperate for me to do so... but he won't do anything other than position himself like this, waiting for me to give him some sign that I'll welcome him inside of me again.

Too many men have wanted to claim me. To own me. That's part of being a sex symbol, I get it, but that's also one of the reasons I've been so choosy about my lovers over the years. I haven't fucked half the men the Internet claims I have, and I stopped doing any kind of social media on my own when I realized that the whole fucking world thinks they deserve a piece of Whiskey Rose.

My looks are constantly up for discussion. Any weight gain or weight loss... the comments are brutal. My lyrics are forever dissected, and while "Heart Barely Used" was the last song I ever wrote about a real-life person I knew, some fans write theses about what phantom lover of mine is the subject of my newer lyrics.

But that's the thing. They want Whiskey Rose.

No one ever wants *Sierra*.

Until now.

Until Dagon.

CHAPTER 17
TIME TO EAT

SIERRA

Earlier tonight, that didn't make sense to me. When he told me that he loved me... that he *knew* me... that I was meant to be his one true mate, I didn't get it. It's been a weekend. That's all. So he knows my body; no denying that. He knows I love my cat, and that I'm so paranoid about stalkers and clingy fans, I wear a disguise to answer my front door.

But it's more than that, isn't it? He knows I hate my feet being cold. I didn't tell him that, and he still held my bare feet in his warm hands while we were watching a movie without any word or complaint from me. He just noticed me tucking my feet under his thigh for heat and moved on to gently caressing the soles of my feet instead.

Apart from when he tried to hunt my poor cat, he's been so good to him.

And now, even though he has to know I'm gagging for him to touch me a little more intimately than just holding onto my waist, he's staying still, waiting for me to invite him in...

He has my essence. I can't take that back any more than I can the promise I made in the heat of the moment. If he can access my thoughts, my dreams, my experiences, my *memories* the same way I've been able to access his, he sure as fuck knows me now.

He knows Whiskey Rose—and he knows Sierra.

He knew that I needed him... and here he is. Naked. *Hot*. He's in my shower with me, where I'm also very naked and incredibly hot.

Fucking him again would be a big mistake. It would tell him that I'm okay with this whole 'bonding' thing. That he really did claim me.

I can't go with him to Sombra, though. He seems to think that, as his mate, I have to, but I *can't*. And if screwing him again in the shower gives him the wrong idea about our future... I shouldn't.

And despite knowing that, it still doesn't stop me from grabbing his cock by the base and putting the tip of him just inside of me.

"I don't want to worry about what's going to happen tomorrow." Like always, I'm going to live in the *now* for as long as I can. And current Sierra? She's going to turn around and climb Dagon like a tree if he doesn't take her from behind right now. "I just want you to fuck me."

"Mating you like this would be my greatest pleasure," he rumbles, dipping his head to press a heated kiss to the side of my neck. At the same time, he increases the pressure on my hips, pinning me in place as he begins to work his cock inside of me.

He's thicker than before. I expected that. Not only does this position have Dagon hitting nerves I didn't even know existed before, but it wasn't a shadow monster who joined me in my shower just now. The massive, red-skinned demon is solid, huge, and scalding hot as he pushes himself a little further inside of me.

I can take it, though. If only because he stretched me out so deliciously earlier, I can take it, and I spur him to push me to my limits by panting his name softly over the spray of the shower hitting the tiles beneath us.

I brace myself, palms flat against the wall. Going up on my tiptoes, I wiggle a little, helping Dagon get seated before he starts to thrust.

But just as he's given me as much as I can take, he grazes my neck with the edge of his fangs, then tells me, "I will take you like this, claiming you in this very rain every time you dare to wash my scent off of your delicious body. That way, the humans will sense you are taken, even if they cannot see me, and I can still warn them away from my mate."

I gasp.

Dagon stills at the sound. Poor guy. He has no idea what his low voice just did to me, does he?

He starts to withdraw. "Have I filled you too completely, my mate? I know I am large, and you are small—"

It's not that.

"Did you mean it?" I ask, arching my back so that I can follow him as he pulls slowly out of me.

"That I will cover you with my scent so completely, every male will instinctively sense that you have a fierce Sombra hunter as your male?" He jerks his hips, finding his way home again as his groin slams into my ass. "Every word, Sierra. I belong to you, too. I want every male to know that to lust after you is to draw the ire of your devoted mate."

I shudder. God, that was so fucking sexy.

He keeps us connected for a moment as I adjust to his size again. Then, once I let out a throaty moan, he starts moving a little more, fucking me faster, rocking into me as I clutch the shower wall with my fingertips.

"That part," I say, panting as he continues to thrust, "yeah, but also how they won't see you. Are you... I thought you were going back to Sombra."

"I was." A low grunt as he braces one hand over my head, hitting a new angle with his thrusts. "But I meant it when I said only if my mate comes with me. I understand now that you must stay. You belong here, Sierra. In this world of lights and noise and your pretty sounds. No one will love you more than I, but there are those who do love you. I would be a selfish male to keep you all to myself. So I will stay. Like Nox... like Sammael... like the artist..." Dagon punctuates these names of other demons with a forceful thrust that has me going up on the balls of my feet as I take him gladly. "I will stay with my mate wherever she is for as long as she'll have me."

And as he grunts louder, harshly rasping my name when he loses control and empties himself inside of me, I have one delirious thought as I find my own pleasure through *his:* as long as I'll have him?

He promised me forever, and I did the same.

And Sierra Landry ain't no liar.

Once we finally leave the shower, I don't bother pulling on sleep clothes. What's the point? What's done is done, I've got a demon mate now, and I'm going to make the most of it.

We towel off—well, Dagon towels me off, then goes from his solid form to shadow and back to dry himself —before he takes my hand gingerly in his, leading me toward the bed.

I expect him to take advantage of his new mate being very wet and incredibly willing. I've discovered that a demon's recovery period is pretty damn quick because, as he guides me to sit, then plops his bulk down beside me, his dick is ready for round three—or is it four?

I lost track, but I'm ready and raring to go.

Dagon, though, uses his strength to position me right where he wants me. With the smallest of pushes, he has me with my back facing him again. I'm not really sure what that's about—until he starts to use his claws to comb out my wet hair.

It's such a sweet gesture, my heart nearly skips a beat. In my experience, the most I can expect from a lover is a little snuggle and some snoring after we're done. Aftercare? Never. Sharing a sexy shower with my demon is one thing, but for him to comb out my hair for me?

I preen, enjoying his touch. I'm already thinking about how I'm going to show him my appreciation when he finishes untangling the knots and, with amazingly dexterous fingers, braids my hair in a simple three-strand plait.

Okay. I know he has my essence now, but is that enough for him to learn how to do my hair like this?

I'm not sure, and after I marvel at the length of my hair, I have to ask, "How did you learn to do this?"

A proud look flashes across his face. "Susanna showed me how."

Susanna.

I'd purposely made myself forget about her. Everything I learned from Dagon's memories told me that their relationship was platonic—especially since Susanna has her own demon mate—but I can't help it. Whether it's rational or not, it bothers me that *I'm* supposed to be his one true mate, but he spent the last, like, thirty years as the bodyguard for another woman.

Worse? He knows it.

Dagon rubs the back of my neck with his thumb. "Are you jealous, my mate?"

He sounds so surprised that I might be.

And, damn it, it's because I *am*.

I shrug, careful not to look at him. "You care for her."

That much is obvious from his memories and his emotions.

He doesn't deny it, either. "Yes. Because, without Susanna, I would not have survived long enough for the gods to bring you into my life."

Oh.

"I owed her my life, but only until I found my mate. Because, when I did, it would belong to her. It belongs to you, Sierra, just as I do."

I glance over my shoulder at him. "Does that make you my bodyguard then?"

I already have plenty. What's one more?

Dagon shows me his fangs in what must be a teasing demon smile. "My mate... no one will protect this body... *pleasure* this body... better than I."

"That's good to know."

His nostrils flare.

Without another word, Dagon takes my braid back in hand before setting it gently over my shoulder. Then, proving he can be just as dominant as he is gentle, my demon takes me by my upper arms, turning me quickly before shifting his hold on me. One big hand braces my lower back, the other clutching my right shoulder, he eases me back onto my bed.

At one heated look from my demon, my legs fall open. He turns his claw to shadow so that he doesn't cut me before trailing his fingertip through the moisture already gathered at the entrance to my core.

He purrs. Seriously. My demon sounds like Three on steroids, the rumble in his chest is so loud and resonant.

Dagon pops his finger into his mouth, licking it clean. His red eyes flare. "So soon, Sierra? Already you need me again?"

Hasn't he learned by now? When it comes to my attraction to him, I will *always* need him. The rest... it'll come in time, I'm sure, but I'd be lying if I said this wasn't a good start.

Hey. He's my one true love. My forever mate. If he

enjoys going down on me as much as I do, I don't see any reason to stop him.

But first—

I hold up a finger, reaching behind me with my other hand. "Give me a second."

"We have an eternity, my mate. But your male is a hungry hunter. He needs to feast."

Sounds good to me. It's just... where did I toss my phone? I know I had it... ah. My fingers close on the familiar glass enclosure. Got it!

Lifting my phone in front of my face, I'm not surprised that Billie hasn't texted me back. It's 9:15, and if she really is on her way back to New York, she won't have anything to say until then.

Just in case, I type out a quick message.

> I might be sleeping when you get back. Just knock if you need me.

Billie might not be bold enough to simply waltz into my room like Jared does, but on the odd chance that she's completely lost her mind tonight, I want to make sure she doesn't see something she shouldn't.

Pressing send, I scurry out of the bed, smiling to myself at Dagon's noticeable growl as I'm suddenly out of his reach.

Sorry, my demon. Just in case... I turn the lock on my door.

There. All better.

He's my mate now, no matter what. And as much as I'm not looking forward to hiding Dagon from my best friend, I haven't changed my opinion on him ending up in a demon jail cell because of me. Of course, that's future Sierra's problem.

Right now?

I toss my phone somewhere on the bed as I climb on top of the mattress again. Snuggling against the wall of pillows in front of my headboard, I crook my finger at my demon.

"Time to eat."

SIERRA

I do eventually fall asleep next to Dagon that night, even if it's not immediately after I sent Billie that text.

Then again, I guess it's more accurate to say that I was squirming and damn near begging for his dick by the time he was done with his feast, and Dagon was up for the task of trying to satiate my own hunger. After, he insisted on cleaning me up when he was done—with his tongue again first, then a washcloth from my bathroom—before curling up next to me, holding me so close, I couldn't imagine spending another night alone in my bed.

There was no knock at my door while I was still conscious enough to notice. I stole a peek at my phone when Dagon went to retrieve the washcloth. Nothing; at least, nothing from Billie. Jared left me his usual rambling apologies that I delete without reading, and there's a check-in message from Roy. I send my head of security a thumbs up emoji, then toss my phone as Dagon's shadow form comes gliding back toward the bed.

Billie probably changed her mind and decided to stick it out with Trev. She did agree to spend the entire long weekend with him, after all, and it takes a lot for her to break her word.

She'll be home sometime tomorrow, I'm sure. Until then, I snuggle into Dagon, enjoying the moment of peace before I let sleep take me.

Smiling against his warm chest, the last thought I remember having is how Dagon's gods got it right. And maybe this all happened so fucking fast, but I've been lonely for too long. I've worked hard my entire life... don't I deserve something that's just for me?

That's my demon mate. He's the perfect partner for an international superstar, too. No one is allowed to see him, just like I treasure any and all of my private time. He can turn to mist and travel with me when I go back on the road, or even stay here with Three if that's what he wants. It's only a flight away from whatever venue I'm at at the moment, right?

Besides, the docs won't clear me to go back on tour until the new year at least. It's mid-November now, and that gives me time to get to know Dagon without relying on the memories he dumped into my head when he gave me his essence.

The tour goes through the summer. Billie has me scheduled for intensive studio time after that, getting ready for my next album, and there's a stack of scripts I've been ignoring in the study, but maybe it's time I take a vacation.

God knows I haven't had a real once since I was... twelve? Younger?

No work. No limelight. No looming obligations on the horizon. Just me and my lusty, possessive monster... and since there's no going back—whether I would if I could or not—it looks like I have forever to enjoy him.

One day at a time, though. Like everything else in my life, I'll take it one day at a time.

I DON'T KNOW WHAT IT IS THAT WAKES ME UP: THE ACT of Dagon disentangling himself from my body and sliding out of bed, or the absence of his body heat once he's gone. It doesn't matter. My hand finds the empty space beside me and, suddenly, my eyes flutter open.

It's dark. The thick curtains covering my windows are designed to shield the lights and sounds from the city below. I'm used to them and can usually tell the difference between the dark of night and the darkness that comes from the black-out curtains.

It's dark because it's late. Or early, I guess, depending on your perspective. When I'm on the road, I'm rarely in bed before two a.m. by the time I finish my show and get back to the hotel. The best part of being on 'vocal rest' is how much I've needed some downtime for both my body and my mental health.

My body is still tender but oh so sated after my night with Dagon. He's the distraction I needed—and he's gone.

No. As I shift in bed, sliding across the sheets as I pull my tossed blanket closer to me, I peer into the darkness of my room and can just about make out the hulking outline of his shadowy shape. Then, as if proving that I could find him anywhere, his head swivels my way, his red eyes blazing.

He's low. My giant mate is crouched a little, motionless except for when he moved his head. Locking eyes with me, he lifts one thick finger to his mouth.

It's the same gesture whether you're a demon or you're human. Hush.

What's going on?

Dagon's voice is barely a rumbled whisper as he says, "There is another Sombra male nearby. I sense him. He's come for me."

What? "But we're bonded. And we didn't break your ruler's stupid law. Why is he here?"

"I don't know, but I'm going to see what it is he is after. Sierra… stay here while I do." Dagon searches the darkness, nodding when he finds something. He lopes over to the stuffed armchair in the corner where Three reluctantly settled down when he realized that Dagon and I were moving too much for him to fit his chonky body on the bed with us. He pats the cat's head, waking him up. "Guard my mate, creature. I trust you."

To my amazement, Three answers Dagon with a deep-throated *mrow* instead of just swatting at him like he does me when I disturb him.

Dagon nods, then slips toward the closed door. After fiddling with his claws for a few seconds, he manages to unlock it. One final look back at me, then he eases it open a few inches before disappearing out into the apartment.

I almost stay. He told me to, and if his hunter instincts have warned him that there's a threat out there coming from one of his people, I should listen.

But what if Billie did come home last night? She might have knocked and I didn't hear her, or decided it was worth it to just head to her room and talk to me in the morning.

What if she sees the other Sombra demon? What if she sees *Dagon*?

I have to warn him. I didn't bother last night

because I was, damn it, I *was* distracted. I guess, with Billie out of town the last few days, it never really occurred to me that I'd have to do something about Dagon being here when no one is allowed to see him.

Especially since I have the sudden reminder popping into my brain that if a human *does*, Dagon will end up in a set of gold chains, being dragged away from me before spending the rest of his immortal life in a dungeon cell.

Shit. I don't know where that certainty comes from. His memories, I bet, but that just makes me even more determined to keep him hidden while I can. I only just got him. I don't want to see him getting taken away for something I could've prevented if I only told him that Billie mentioned coming home early.

Is that why there's another demon in my apartment? I haven't touched that spellbook in days, so I know I didn't somehow invite another one here, especially since Dagon's made it clear that he only gets one true mate and I'm it. He was careful to keep out of Jared's sight. Same thing when the concierges brought up our delivery orders.

What's going on?

I don't know—but I'm going to find out.

Just in case, I pause only to grab the first robe I can find in my walk-in closet. It's slinky and light, sending a shiver through me as I tug it on, but it's better than walking into my living room bare-assed naked.

I echo Dagon, telling Three to stay behind. My cat yawns, then lays his furry chin on his paws. He's fast asleep in seconds.

Tying my robe together with the sash, I tiptoe out of my bedroom.

I don't see Dagon at first. I don't see Billie, either, or anyone else. A little light streams in through the window that overlooks the street on the east side of the Dorado. The study is empty.

Moving quickly yet silently, I head to the kitchen.

Because Billie insisted on turning the fancy dining room into a study/library for us instead, we keep a small circular table in the kitchen for us to eat. It's not like we ever really use the oven or the stove anyway, but the room is perfect for when we have a rare moment to sit down together and eat a full meal together.

Since Billie's been gone, I've been eating in the living room with Dagon. It was so nice to drop the act of being Whiskey Rose; Sierra enjoys eating out of take-out containers while watching television, and with Dagon, I could do that. The kitchen table hasn't been used in days. It should be empty.

It isn't.

Frowning, I reach for the bag plopped down on top of the table, near Billie's usual seat. For all her level-headed business-mindedness, my manager has one weakness: designer handbags. She has a different one for nearly every outfit, and if it's the only way I can show her how much I appreciate her friendship over the years, I make sure she always has another one to add to her collection.

I recognize this one. It's a large black Prada tote, perfect for a weekend getaway. I bought it as one of Billie's Christmas gifts last year. This has to be hers... and it wasn't here earlier.

Just in case, I peek inside. If it *is* Billie's, she won't give a shit that I did. If it isn't, I have a much bigger problem on my hands than snooping around in some stranger's bag.

There's a phone on top. Tapping the screen, I bring it to life. The picture in the background is of me and Billie during the premiere for *Jessica's Journey*. She has her arms around me, her wild curls almost giving me a halo. My stylist insisted that I swap out my trademark braid for an elaborate updo—a way to show the world there was more to me than the pop star princess—and this moment with Billie was the only time I really smiled the whole night.

I remember that. My co-star in the movie was a handsy bastard who was all for a public showmance during the PR tour. He'd been around the block enough to know that—until Dagon—I still kinda had a thing going with my ex, and that didn't bother him; in fact, I'm pretty sure Colin liked the idea of rubbing a relationship with me in Jared's face.

No, thanks. As 'Jessica', I had to kiss Colin's character more than enough to know I didn't want to continue to do so. Of course, the producers insisted on partnering us up for every interview, every appearance... and I had to do it all with a smile on my face.

Billie always stays in the shadows. The night of the premiere, though? She was my date on the red carpet, and the public goddamn gobbled it up. They didn't need to know that Billie's been my manager and partner in crime these last fifteen years. Seeing two of the three original members of Thr33peat reunite was more than enough fodder to knock any rumors about Colin and me out of the news for the night.

It was so much fun. I have one of the photogs' shots printed out for myself, but Billie made it her background.

Because this... this is her phone.

My stomach sinks to the floor. All of my good memories about that night vanish as the realization that I'm holding Billie's phone in my hand slaps me upside the head.

When I can get away with it, I ignore my phone. There are so many demands on me and my time; the few moments I spend without that sucker glued to my palm, the better. As my manager, though, Billie doesn't get that luxury. Not that I demand her to always be accessible. Oh, no. She *insists*.

She's never without her phone. Her purse, either,

but her phone... even if she went to bed and left her purse out on the table, she'd take her phone with her.

But she hasn't.

Where is she?

Maybe... maybe something really went down between her and Trevor tonight. Billie is so methodical, so meticulous, so organized that it would have to take a lot to rattle her. Rattle her enough that she'd abandon her phone and hide out in her room?

I guess it's *possible*... and I need to go check.

Dagon can handle the other demon. Me? I'm going to go make sure Billie's okay.

In our apartment, there are three bedrooms: mine, Billie's, and the much smaller one that Roy uses when we're amping up security during our stay at the Dorado. Roy's is what used to be called a 'maid's room', positioned off of the kitchen, the furthest room in the apartment. To get to Billie's, I have to cross through the gallery, passing by the living room in order to hit the hall that conceals the door to her bedroom on the other side.

And that's what I do.

I walk toward the living room—and freeze when something catches my eye.

It's Dagon.

My demon is still faded to mist. His eyes are two barely-there reddish pinpricks hovering in the space in that same predatory crouch as before, back in the bedroom.

I don't think he notices me. He has one hand low to the hardwood floor, claws outstretched. The other is hanging in front of his groin. His head is bowed, hair shoved down his back as he watches something just out of my sight.

He's a hunter. He told me that from the beginning. In Sombra, his job used to be finding meat and hunting it, providing for the village. After he pledged his life to protecting *Susanna*, he hunted for threats to the duke's mate—but seeing him now, I'm stunned by how fierce he is.

Fierce and super fucking sexy.

Only one problem. If Dagon is in hunt mode, that leaves me with one very important question: who is he hunting?

Another Sombra demon would see him. Humans never expect to find real monsters in the shadows, so they won't be able to pick Dagon's form out of nothingness. I can because he's my mate, but if he's facing off against the demon he sensed out here...

I have to look. I don't want to distract him, but I have to know.

Inching forward, I grab the edge of the opening that leads into the living room, poking my head out just far enough to see a figure sitting on the far cushion of my favorite settee.

I gasp. I'd do anything to take the sound back because it doesn't only snare Dagon's attention. The second I suck in that breath, the male lurking in my living room turns toward me, and I get a perfect look at his profile.

That's not a demon.

That's *Trevor*.

I'VE ONLY MET TREVOR DANIELS A HANDFUL OF TIMES.

Makes sense. Billie doesn't bring anyone around me until she's comfortable enough to let them know that she isn't just my manager, but my de facto older sister and best friend. In Trev's case, that took almost eight months. In the four months since, between the kick-off to my tour and spending six weeks on set, I've spent maybe a couple of hours with Billie's boyfriend.

I don't blame her for being cautious. Over the years, too many people have used her to try and get close to me. It's one of the reasons why I'm so protective of her. She's one of the best things that has ever happened to me, and it kills me whenever someone hurts her because they're more interested in the figment of Whiskey Rose than getting to know what an amazing person Billie Bickles is.

Trevor seemed to pass the test. Our few meetings have left little impression on me, mainly because he barely said 'hello'. He was so enchanted by Billie it was like I wasn't even there. The guy couldn't even make eye contact with me; he was too busy watching her.

That's why it was such a surprise and a bit disappointing when Billie started mentioning she might be ending things with Trev soon. I had thought they were such a good match, but maybe not.

Or Maybe I got the wrong idea from her texts. I assumed something went down with her boyfriend, but it's possible they both decided to return to Manhattan a day earlier instead of sticking it out in Connecticut.

I'm so relieved. If Trevor's here, that means Billie must be, too. She's got to be in her room, grabbing something, and her boyfriend is waiting for her out here. There's probably a good reason why she plopped her purse and her phone in the kitchen, too, but the clock over the stove said it was 4:04 in the morning, and maybe I'm just too tired to come up with what it could be.

Trevor's even wearing his winter coat. They either must have just gotten in or are on their way out again because why else is he sitting in my living room, wearing a winter coat?

A small, shy smile curves his lips when he sees me standing in the open doorway. His gaze dips just enough to notice the silhouette of me in my slinky robe—and his smile widens.

My relief dies a very quick death when I see that.

"Trevor." Going along with the facade that I'm 'resting', I keep my voice low... but not so low that Billie won't hear me speaking if she's one room over. "What are you doing here?"

He pushes off of the settee, turning so that he's facing me. "Did I wake you? I would've waited until morning if I had to."

Waited? For what?

To his left, Dagon shifts his bulk, still hiding in the faint shadows as he continues to watch the human male as intently as Trevor watches *me*.

I cross my arm over my chest, trying my best to hide my sudden nerves—and my near-nakedness. "That's okay. Um, I thought I heard Billie. Where is she? Her room?"

Trevor shrugs. His hands are in his coat pockets, I notice. "I'm not sure actually. I was hoping I beat her back to New York, and I thought I had when I came up here and couldn't find anyone awake. I didn't bother you, but her room was empty. The study, too. In fact, I haven't seen her since we got separate cars back to the city, and that was around midnight."

Midnight. And Billie's the one who told me hours before that that she was planning on heading back to Manhattan.

What did her last message say? Something about

having to do something else first, and we'd talk about it later.

Uh-oh. I swallow nervously, wondering if I should just make a break for my bedroom where I trust my lock… or pretend like I don't suddenly have a real bad feeling about all of this.

Maybe I'm not as good an actress as all the reviews about *Jessica's Journey* said because Trevor immediately can tell I'm not falling for whatever crap he's selling.

He cocks his head slightly. "Hey. Is everything okay?"

What are you doing here without your girlfriend? "Yeah. Of course. What about you? You and Billie okay?"

"Everything's great, Whiskey."

And, yup, that does it all right.

CHAPTER 19

TREVOR AND BILLIE

SIERRA

Panic flares up inside of me so quickly, I nearly stumble backward.

Whiskey…

Everyone in my inner circle knows better than to address me by my stage name. Even Jared sticks to calling me 'Rosie', never 'Whiskey', while everyone else uses 'Sierra'. I know that Billie introduced me to Trevor with my real name… so why the hell did he just call me 'Whiskey' like that?

"I'm glad. And I'm sure Billie will be here soon." *Where is she? Her purse is here. Her phone is here. He's here…* "If you don't mind, I'm going back to bed. I don't usually get up this early—"

"I know. When you're on tour, you get up by eight

in the morning so that you can eat a healthy breakfast, then get two hours of exercise in to keep your shape. When you're not in the middle of a project, you prefer to sleep in to ten and call yourself lazy when you do."

Those words... they came from Trevor, but that's only because he just parroted something I've said in nearly every health mag-related interview I've given over the last five years.

Women age. Men do, too, but they're not given shit for it. The public has this idea of me as the half-dressed sixteen-year-old I was, gracing the covers of every industry pub. A decade into the biz, they turned on me for the sole crime of reaching my mid-twenties.

I had to reinvent myself. I was getting older, my body was changing, and I went through a period where I loathed myself for it. It was Billie who reminded me that Whiskey Rose could belong to Sierra Landry as much as the rest of the world. So I released my third album, changed my style completely to prove that I was growing up, and got into fitness to attempt to hang on to my twenty-year-old body.

It didn't really work. I mean, I look good at thirty-one. No denying that. But so long as I said the right things, letting the public think I was *trying*, they gave me a small pass.

I gave that up a couple of years ago when I realized that while my fans were aging, too, I was also getting younger and younger girls looking up to me. How could I expect them to love themselves when I couldn't love *myself*? So I tweaked my image again because I wanted to, and the tone of some of my fan mail slowly but surely began to change.

Except for the creep letters, of course. From fans so obsessed with the idea of Whiskey Rose they could parrot years-old interviews right back at me as if they're fact, and not something I made up on a whim once and ran with.

But Billie's boyfriend… he's not a fan.

Right?

I didn't think so. But the way he's looking at me from across the room?

I'm not so sure anymore.

"I wouldn't call you lazy, Whiskey. Everything you've accomplished in your career… you're the opposite of lazy."

"Um. Thank you, Trevor."

"You're welcome. I've been waiting a long, long time to tell you that. I think you're amazing."

You've gotta be fucking kidding me.

"Billie tells me you're a great guy, too," I tell him.

"That's why I had to beat her here, you know. I didn't want to give her a chance to poison you against me. Not until you know how I really felt."

I swallow roughly, trying to hide how uncomfortable I am, then say softly, "And how's that?"

Instead of answering me, he shuffles a few steps closer to me. "Did you get my letters?"

What? Letters? "I, um, I don't think so."

Trevor snorts in annoyance. "Figures. I knew you'd write me back if you did. I asked Billie last week if they made it to you. She wouldn't answer."

Of course she wouldn't.

Trevor wrote me letters... is that why she suggested I go through my fan mail? If I hadn't, I never would've found the spellbook that brought me Dagon... but did Billie know about Trevor being another one of my obsessed fans?

No. She couldn't. She's actually the one who tried to separate any letters that looked questionable...

A lump lodges in my throat. Did she know? Did she find a letter... *letters*... that looked familiar enough that she began to doubt her own boyfriend? Did Trevor tip her off by asking about them? He said last week—and that was around the time Billie started questioning her relationship with him.

Is this why?

"Did Billie know? About"—I swallow the lump roughly, wincing as it bothers my throat—"your feelings for me?"

"That I'm in love with you?"

Oh, God. "Yes."

"I think she guessed. She's not really the jealous type, but she seemed suspicious when I would ask about you. I don't know why. She doesn't own Whiskey Rose. Whiskey Rose belongs to all of us."

Damn it. He really is another nutcase. Just as bad as Patrick Ridgefield, too. Because while that cuckoo fan followed me everywhere before stealing my cat and breaking up one of my relationships, he drew his weapon in a crowd outside. I had security who saved me then, and Patrick's supposedly locked up where he can't hurt me ever again.

But Trevor...

Trevor Daniels pretended to be another nice guy. He acted like he couldn't give two shits about me being Whiskey Rose whenever we met. But, all along, he was using Billie to get as close as possible to me without tipping any of us off—and it fucking *worked*.

Look at this asshole. Instead of being with her in Connecticut, he's standing here in our apartment without her.

I can't even blame a lapse in my security for this. As Billie's boyfriend for the last *year*, of course he's on the list to visit us. The Dorado security team would've waved him on in earlier tonight, not even thinking of informing Roy about our late-night visitor, and they would've just been doing their duty.

Now? Fuck me, but now I'm in the same room as this creep, I have no idea where Billie is, and my demon mate... he's watching the exchange without a word, unable to help me because he can't let Trevor see him.

Yup. I'm fucked.

Do you think I have my phone on me? I can't even send an SOS to Roy for help because I stupidly left it back in bed. Thank God I grabbed a robe, but the way Trevor is basically undressing me with his dark eyes, it's pretty much useless.

"Trevor—"

"Whiskey Rose belongs to all of us," he says, drawing his right hand out of his pocket, "but you're going to be *mine*."

Holy shit. He didn't just pull his hand out of his pocket.

He pulled out a *gun*.

I go motionless. Not like I was really moving much before, but staring down the barrel of his gun... suddenly thrown back to the day outside of the theater... I don't move a goddamn muscle.

"I'm sorry, Whiskey. I know this must be giving you flashbacks to Ridgefield, and if there was any other way, I wouldn't have gone for a gun. But I... I'm desperate, okay? This is the only thing I could think to do to get your attention."

Oh, really? Well, yeah, but that's because it fucking works, dickhead.

Even as he tries to explain himself aiming a gun

dead at my chest, I'm completely frozen in place. I can't move. I can barely *breathe*. I'm useless.

But my amazing demon isn't.

Slowly pulling himself up to his full height, he blends in with the shadows as he shifts away from Trevor and his weapon.

I try my best not to follow his trajectory with my gaze. The last thing I need right now is Trevor noticing and asking me what I'm doing.

I'm in trouble, but that doesn't mean Dagon has to be.

And the crazy bastard is still talking...

"I didn't want to do this." Trevor's voice turns pleading as he keeps his steady hand and his gun trained on me. "You can blame Billie for that. I went to all that trouble to plan a weekend away for her. Basically *begged* her to go with me... all because she was pulling away from me. I could tell, you know. She was getting ready to end it. But I couldn't let her do that. Not when I'd lose any access I had to you before I could show you we're meant to be together. And what does she do? Ask me point-blank who I loved. Was I supposed to lie?"

I don't know what to say, but since the crazy bastard with the gun seems to want an answer to his question, I give him the one he seems to want to hear.

"Of course not."

"Exactly! Billie was fine, but she was always

number two. She's not Whiskey Rose. She'll never be number one."

Technically, if we're talking about Thr33peat now, I'm number three. Tandy was number one, though it's not like I'm about to correct him.

Instead, I scrounge up as much of a smile as I can. "I'm touched you feel that way. But I'm—"

I never get to finish my sentence.

Jerking the gun, closing the gap between us in a few frantic strides, spit flies from Trevor's mouth as he snaps. "Don't you dare try to tell me we can't be together. That your heart still belongs to Jared fucking Turner. You sang it yourself. Your heart was barely used after he tried to break it. He doesn't deserve you."

Trevor's not wrong. Jared doesn't deserve me, but that doesn't mean *we* can be together. Even if he wasn't an obsessed weirdo who pulled a gun on me or the man my best friend's been dating for a year, he isn't *my* one true love.

My one true love is slinking along the far wall, heading toward the fireplace, moving with such purpose, I really hope he has a plan...

"It's not Jared—"

"Don't lie to me, Whiskey!"

My mouth clamps shut as his roar echoes around me.

Trevor is breathing heavily. His finger is mere centimeters from the trigger on his gun, and I'm back to being a frozen stiff. One wrong move and he's firing the gun—and the only thing separating us is the settee between me and Trevor.

He exhales again, his voice is a lot calmer now. "I've seen him. Lurking around the Dorado, hoping you'll let him up to see you. I kept my mouth shut, but not anymore. You're mine. Now get dressed. You're coming home with me."

I honestly have no idea how Trevor thinks this is going to work. Like it or not, I have one of the most recognizable faces in the world. He could try marching me out of the Dorado, but if the cameras don't catch me leaving, someone will. With as many celebs who pay the big bucks for privacy inside the building, there's usually a handful of paps outside at any given hour, just hoping for a chance sighting on our way out.

I guess you can't reason with crazy, though, because Trevor honestly seems to think I'm just going to willingly leave with him.

And I'm not sure if the gun he's pointing at me would've been enough for him to get me to, and I'll never know, either, because of what happens next.

As terrified as I am, I catch sight of Dagon materializing just enough that his shadows mingle with those in the far corner of the living room.

He grabs something shiny from the mantle over the empty fireplace. One of my Grammy awards, I think.

And a heavy one at that.

Trevor's not allowed to see Dagon. I don't know why I thought that meant my mate would just stand there and let him threaten me. To be fair, I'm not even sure that Dagon knows enough about human weaponry to understand the damage a gun can do from this close of a distance. If he tapped into my life experiences, he probably does, but that's not what kicked him into gear.

Nope. It's hearing another male try to claim me as his when Dagon already did.

My possessive demon is even quicker than the insane human. Before Trevor can do anything but waggle the gun in my direction again, Dagon raises the heavy trophy up high, then brings it down on Trevor's head.

The gun falls out of his hand first, clattering against the floor; thankfully, it doesn't go off. Trevor crumples up next, falling face-first on my floor as Dagon drops his arm to his side before materializing completely in his red-skinned, solid form.

Scurrying around the side of the settee, I stop when I'm a few feet away from his body.

"Is he dead?"

Dagon eases my blood-covered Grammy—for Best New Artist—onto the floor, then lowers his body so that he can prod Trevor's cheek with the edge of his claw. When that doesn't do anything, he clutches the human man by the shoulder, flipping him onto his back.

Trev's head hits the floor with a *clunk*. I'm pretty sure that was on purpose, and if he isn't dead, that will only add to the head injury he has.

Dagon bends over him, waiting a moment before he rests back on his heels.

"He is breathing," he announces.

I exhale roughly, and Dagon's eyes shine brightly.

"I can end him now. A mercy this male does not deserve, but I will do that if you ask of me."

"Wait— kill him? Oh, shit. No. Don't do that, Dagon. He's out, but I don't want him *dead*."

How would I ever explain that to Billie? This is bad enough... but murder? Demons might treat life differently, especially a hunter, but I'm a coddled pop star. Life has never felt so real as it does at this moment— and neither does *forever*.

I'm immortal now. That's what Dagon told me. If I got shot, would I have died? What about Dagon? When he's in his shadows, I can still touch him. Would a bullet hurt him?

Hmm... maybe I should let him finish Trevor off.

No. "We have jails here." Thinking of his memories, I amend it to, "Dungeons. Police. They'll take care of this asshole."

"Or you could let me prove myself as a hunter to you. This is just another part of the hunt, my mate. If you'd rather I didn't use my claws, I can bring him to Sombra and let the shadows have him." Dagon gentles his harsh voice. "He will never frighten you again."

I can't do that. I mean, I kinda want to, but I *can't*.

"That's okay. He didn't see you, so we didn't break your duke's law or anything. If he comes to, he'll just remember getting konked on his head. He won't know who did it. I'll say it was me."

I might take a hit to my rep when it inevitably gets out. Then again, Whiskey Rose fighting off an obsessed stalker on her own, braining him with my Grammy? There's a better chance it'll only increase my popularity...

Dagon is watching me with a curious expression on his striking features. I don't know when I started to be able to read him as well as I can—though, to be fair, his essence definitely helps—but he seems touched.

Like he never expected that I would offer to take the fall for something he did.

I have to. Not only because I've come too far to sacrifice my tie to Dagon so soon, but because someone has to take care of this—and Billie... that's usually something Billie would do.

And I still don't know if she's here or not.

Forget Trevor for a second. Before he stole my attention from what I was doing, I was looking for Dagon and Billie. And Dagon... he was looking for another demon.

Lunging toward Dagon, I drop to my knees at his side and clutch his arm. "You said there was another demon. That's why you were out here."

"Glaine, yes. One of Duke Haures's top guards. I sensed him before." Running his shadowy hand over my trembling back, assuring himself I'm still here, Dagon lifts me up so that we're both standing again. "There was a portal, different from the one that brought me here. By the time I tracked it, it had winked out again. Glaine's essence lingered, though, so I sought him out. But when I checked your quarters, I found the human male waiting for you first and no Glaine."

I pointedly refuse to look down at Trevor again. He's not dead—for now—and me saving him from whatever shadows Dagon mentioned is all that he deserves from me. "Where was the portal?"

My demon hesitates. I don't think he wants to leave Trevor alone, but he must realize that the bastard's not going anywhere, either.

"Come with me, my mate." Keeping his hand on my back, he leads the way for us until we're both standing in the kitchen. He points at the refrigerator. "Here. It opened right in front of your large rectangle."

A Sombra demon appeared in the middle of my kitchen—and Billie's purse was left unattended on the table...

I swallow roughly, trying not to let my imagination

run away from me. There has to be a logical explanation, right? I mean, 'logical' probably flew out the fucking window when Billie's boyfriend pulled a gun on me... but, hey. Tonight can't get any worse, can it?

"He was here? This Glaine?"

"Yes."

And though I'm pretty sure I already know the answer to my question, I ask, "Where is he now?"

Is he hiding in the shadows? I can see Dagon's outline even when he's mist because he's *mine*. Is this other demon... Glaine... is he hiding? I didn't get to finish searching for Billie, and maybe Dagon got interrupted from tracking down Glaine when he stumbled upon Trevor—

With a sorrowful shake of his head, my demon says, "He is gone."

And after one final search throughout the apartment, I have to admit that so is Billie.

SIERRA

All I want to do is go after Billie.

If I wasn't Whiskey Rose, I could have. But with Trevor's unconscious body in my living room, and the inevitable fallout from another stalker getting past my security... I couldn't just go. Not when I have every intention of sticking around through the last of my commitments for my fans' sake.

It would be so much easier if I could accept Dagon's offer to disappear the creep. If only. Between the cameras and the guards, there's proof that Trevor came up to the apartment. The last thing I need now is Trevor going missing and the media getting their hands on video footage that shows him walking into my apartment building, but not walking out again.

Besides, after the way he so boldly pulled a gun on me, I want him behind bars. I'll throw the full weight of my legal team at him if I have to, and after I call Roy and he shows up with a couple of his guys in no time, my lawyer, Charlotte, is the next contact I dial. She's hot on his heels, arriving right after Roy.

And, thanks to Roy taking point on this, so do New York's finest.

Despite my head of security insisting that the cops would do their best to be discreet, I've got a line of squad cars outside as the winter sun is rising, and at least three officers slyly asking for my autograph in between the EMTs checking Trevor over and Roy barking instructions at his crew.

Forcing the old familiar smile to my face, I sign whatever scraps of paper they shove in my face while Dagon lurks in the shadows, lingering close by me while almost completely hidden from the rest of the humans infiltrating my apartment.

I tell my story once, then turn on the waterworks when a different cop wants me to go through it again and again. Charlotte does what Billie usually would, stepping in and informing the detective that—technically—I'm still supposed to be on vocal rest. As my legal counsel, she would field any questions with the help of my head of security.

Between Roy and Charlotte, I'm shielded as the rest of the cops do whatever it is they're paid to. A couple are sent to review the camera footage, and I overhear one telling the cop in charge that a curly-haired blonde in a red dress came in about an hour before Trevor did.

Billie.

I made it clear that the only reason Trevor got past security in the first place was because of his relationship with my best friend and manager. On the outside, it seems like she came home around two a.m., with Trevor slipping into the building a little after three. It was just after four when Dagon woke up and, following my mate out of our room, I found Trevor sitting on my settee.

They don't ask about Billie; at least, they don't ask *me.* When Roy let the cops know that she was already gone by the time I confronted Trevor, it seemed like there was no reason to question her for the moment. I'm sure they'll need to eventually, especially since she was with Trevor before he snapped and went nuts on me, but he was still out when the paramedics loaded him up on a stretcher, leaving a pool of blood and his gun behind on my hardwood floor.

One cop bagged up his weapon as evidence before following after the stretcher. Roy noticed the blood, then snagged Gino, instructing him to clean it up once the detective gave him the okay. Charlotte got a laundry list of possible charges to press against Trevor before arranging to meet with the detective down at NYPD headquarters to make sure they go through with throwing the book at him.

Roy sends Gino and Jeff home after everyone finally clears out. Once it's just the two of us—and Dagon, though Roy has no idea that my mate is hovering right over his shoulder—Roy asks me if I want him to stick around until Billie comes back. Like the cops, he's sure that she must've snuck out of the apartment, careful to avoid the cameras, once she knew Trevor had followed her home.

Roy is as fond of Billie as he is of me. They've both been in my inner circle for more than a decade, and I can tell he's either worried that Billie's in trouble—or that, somehow, she betrayed me by selling me out to her bastard of a boyfriend.

She would never. Though I have nothing more to go on than my gut feeling and knowing that Sombra demons exist, it's so much easier for me to believe that Billie got mixed up in the paranormal over her selling me out to Trevor. Something had to have happened to her. To leave her purse and her phone behind... something happened.

Dagon agrees with me. As I played my part, the gracious celebrity who was so sorry that my infamy was causing everyone so much trouble, my protective demon kept sending me pulses of affection through our newly forged bond. He wants me to know he's there, that he's not going anywhere, and that he'll do whatever it takes to help me.

Including bringing me to Sombra to search for Billie once I finally convince Roy to go.

WAY I SEE IT, WE HAVE NO CHOICE. CAMERAS DON'T LIE.

Well, no. With the right angle and the proper lighting, fuck yeah, they can lie. But when the security footage shows Billie coming up to the penthouse, but not going back down again... so my team is convinced she found a way to sneak out. So the cops were too dazzled by being called to Whiskey Rose's private apartment to give a shit about the missing 'manager'... something happened to her, and even Dagon is convinced that it has something to do with the other Sombra demon he sensed just outside of the bedroom.

Now that we're bonded, Dagon can open a portal between his world and mine. I don't ask too many questions. There's no time. Based on what I've picked up from his essence, there's a pathway that only exists because I summoned him with the *verus amor* spell. The guard who snuck into my apartment would've needed a demon wizard to let him in unless Billie somehow summoned him—and since the big, leather-bound spell book has been in my room since I opened that fateful package, that couldn't have happened.

I just wish I knew what *did* happen...

Our only chance is to go straight to the top: Duke Haures himself.

I didn't need Dagon's essence to learn about him. My demon had told me plenty while we were first getting to know each other. He's the reason why the human world and demon realm are kept separate—and also the hypocritical mate of the human woman that Dagon spent the last couple of decades serving.

Not gonna lie... I'm not too keen on meeting this Susanna chick. Right before he waves his hand, opening the portal into Sombra, Dagon assures me that I probably won't even see her. Duke Haures is as overprotective of his mate as mine is of me, and he usually keeps her tucked out of sight in his palace.

And considering I made her former bodyguard *mine*... without Dagon shadowing her, she's probably hidden away.

Here's hoping.

I've never seen an actual demon portal before. When Dagon first arrived on Earth, I was in another room, so I had no idea what they looked like until my mate lowers his brawny arm, looking down at me with an expectant expression.

He wants me to like what I see. More than that, he wants me to be proud of him—and to do whatever he can to help me track down my friend.

My first glimpse of Sombra is at odds with some of

Dagon's memories I've already caught flashes of. So many of them are tinged with red, showing me a fiery world with black shadows, ash, and a red moon. The portal itself is about eight feet high and three feet wide, and while there's no denying the hazy shadows that dance in the rectangle-shape in front of me, everything else is... blue?

"Mavro," rumbles Dagon. "This portal will bring us right to Duke Haures's palace in the capital city. If anyone knows why Glaine visited the human world, then left again so suddenly, it'll be his grace."

Right. Because this Glaine guy is the head soldier in the duke's retinue of guards—and because no one comes and goes between the two realms without the ruler of Sombra knowing about it.

Dagon was allowed to because I'm his one true mate. If any other human had learned he was there, the duke would've sent his soldiers after his ass... but he didn't. There was no reason why another Sombra demon should've been in my place. Dagon says there was one, though, and I believe him—and, so far, that's the best lead I have on finding Billie.

"And we just... what? Hop in?"

"Yes."

I take Dagon's hand in mine... or as much of it as I can. "Let's go."

He steps first, his gentle grip on my fingers tugging me after him. It's dark in here, blasted with a dry heart so suddenly that I feel like I've stepped out beneath the outdoor warmers that surround my building during the winter. I gasp, but Dagon doesn't stop. Because he doesn't, neither do I.

Another step and the heat is gone. It's nowhere near as cold as mid-November in New York, though the chill in the air is enough to make me wish I'd grabbed a hoodie before we left. The floor beneath my flats is slippery, almost like glass, and when I glance down to see where I've landed, I see it's made of crystal.

So is the massive throne that's perched on top of a dais that stands about three feet off the ground where I'm standing with Dagon.

The room is blue. Probably because the ceiling over our head is partially open, the dark sky and the hanging moon are both made up of a vivid blue color, and it reflects on the crystal decorations that cover this elegant throne room.

Because, yup. That's a throne, and the oversized demon wearing the crown who's sitting on it... he's definitely Sombra royalty.

Duke Haures is even more intimidating in real life. The pale-skinned demon with shocking blue eyes glowing out of his face is a good head taller than even Dagon, with a body that would put an NFL linebacker to shame. His crystalline crown sits on top of his strikingly white hair, and instead of fangs like Dagon's, he has *tusks* growing up and over his top lip.

He's lounging on his throne, legs spread slightly, large bare feet braced against the floor. He's bare-chested, too, a slight shimmer on his eerily pale skin that gets lost in the sculpted muscles. Instead of wearing shadowy leathers like my demon, his bottom half is covered in white pants that flare out over his ankles.

God bless his tailor, right?

I know from Dagon's memories that the duke is a volatile creature. He's been in charge of the Sombra demons for two thousand years now, and he rules his realm with an iron—or, I don't know now, maybe *crystal*—fist. I need him to want to help me because if he chooses not to... I'm fucked.

And Billie might be in big, big trouble.

I have to believe she's here. If she isn't... no. Billie's in this demon world, and I'm gonna get her out.

Hey. I'm Whiskey Rose. Sierra might be an insecure mess, but when I'm Whiskey, there isn't anything I can't accomplish if I put my mind to it.

Grammy awards. A movie gig. Sold-out tours, number one hits, even turning the tabloids against Jared for cheating on me the first time... I toss my trademark braid over my shoulder, give the demon duke my most photogenic smile, and hope like hell that he can be charmed the same way half the human population has been over my career.

To my surprise, his gaze flickers over me, dismissing me just as quickly. And as conceited as it sounds, I'm so unused to being ignored that I'm speechless for a moment as he turns his attention back to my mate.

"You returned sooner than expected." Duke Haures's glowing blue eyes lift toward the open ceiling. I follow it and notice the sliver of gold hanging up in the sky near the bluish moon. "The gold moon won't rise for another cycle, but I see you've brought your mortal mate with you." His nostrils flare. "And that you've made her your forever mate."

That's right. Mortal? Not anymore, buddy.

Before I can point that out, Dagon eases his big body in front of me. I can tell that part of that is because he wants to protect me—even from his ruler—and part of it is because he wants to keep the dangerous duke's attention on himself.

Dagon genuflects. "My lord. This is my mate. Sierra Landry of the human world."

I wave. "Hi. Anyway, we have a reason why we're here—"

"I'm certain you do. But that can wait."

Uh, no. I don't think it can. "It's just—"

Duke Haures gestures with his hand. Another demon—this one with green eyes—materializes out of the shadows in the corner behind the dais. He's in the inky black shape that Dagon uses when he wants to move quickly—and this demon does, appearing just behind the throne in a heartbeat.

"Harth. Bring my mate to me."

The demon bobs his head, showing off a pair of horns that are more of a corkscrew shape than both Dagon's and the duke's. In the blink of an eye, he's crossing the room, reaching for a door that blends so seamlessly into the wall, I never saw it.

Then he's gone, and Duke Haures grins at Dagon.

Well, I think he's grinning... though it's more like he bares his oversized teeth at him.

"Su would never forgive me if I didn't inform her you brought your mate with you to Mavro."

Su... wonderful.

All I want to do is find Billie, but it looks like I'm going to have to meet Susanna first.

EPILOGUE

SIERRA

I don't want to be the jealous girlfriend. I never have. When Jared gave up being exclusive with me because he just couldn't resist Tandy, I decided then and there that I would never be jealous again. If I couldn't keep him on my own, I didn't want him—and when Jared came crawling back, I used him for my own pleasure, then let him know we'd never be more than FWB ever again.

This is different. Whether Fate said so, or it was magic, or I've just hit the point in my life that I'm ready to settle down... it doesn't matter. Dagon is my true love. He promised himself to me. His type of demon is hardwired to be loyal, and he'll never cheat.

Does that mean I don't immediately compare

myself to the other human woman who means so much to him?

I wish it did.

This would be so much easier if Susanna Benoit was a Whiskey Rose fan. Slipping into my pop star persona, I'd exude the confidence I'm known for. Kind of hard to do that when Susanna is a brunette beauty with a timeless face and a body that I spend hours every week in the Dorado's private gym to attain.

Unfortunately, when I think 'timeless', I'm right. Though she looks younger than me in person, I know from Dagon's essence that she's been Duke Haures's mate and consort for at least thirty human years now. Immortality looks good on her since she can't be more than twenty-five.

Her expression lights up when she sees Dagon standing in front of the duke's throne. When she sees me, her lips form an 'O' in surprise—but definitely not recognition. Of course not. While sometimes it seems like I've been in the biz for an eternity, Thr33peat only became well-known about fifteen years ago. She'd already been in Sombra for that long by then, and she has no idea who I am.

No. That's not right. She knows exactly who I am: Dagon's mate.

Once she reaches the throne, she stands at her mate's side, laying both of her hands on his meaty arm.

The 'O' flattens, then widens as a grin turns her from beautiful to stunning.

I swallow back my envy. She's the duke's mate, I remind myself, and Dagon is mine. He only cared for her because he believed she saved his life out in the shadows. He never loved her the way he loves me...

...because he loves me. It hits me in a rush, cutting through my constant worry for Billie and the thick jealousy that has me in a chokehold.

He loves me, and I inch out from behind his bulk, mimicking Susanna's possessive hold on her mate by clutching Dagon's arm.

"Dagon. I'm so happy to see that you found your mate. I've wanted that for you for so long." She turns her smile on me. Now, I know fake smiles. I use them all the time myself. Two-faced witches are standard in my industry, and I like to think I can spot them. Susanna... she's being entirely genuine as she says, "Welcome to Sombra. It's time we added another human woman to our world."

Oh. Uh. No.

I shake my head at the same time as Dagon clears his throat. "Thank you for welcoming my mate, Susanna, but I've chosen to follow in Nox's path. Sammael, too. Until my mate chooses to spend forever in Sombra with me, I will join her life in the human world."

Forever... eventually, we'll have to live here. I know

that. I live in the public eye, and while money and plastic surgery can go a long way to explain why I look so damn young over the next couple of years, eventually someone will notice that I'm not aging. I mean, Susanna here is proof that immortality means living forever just as I am. I figure I have ten, maybe fifteen years before someone questions it... and that's if I want to be Whiskey Rose for that much longer.

For now, though, I plan on finishing my tour, promoting my next movie, and recording at least one more album; full of love songs this time, I'm thinking. *I Give Myself to You* has a nice ring to it, and so does *Meant to Be Mine...*

Of course, none of that matters while my manager —and my best friend—is inexplicably missing, but I still don't get the chance to ask about her because Duke Haures is currently pointing one super long black claw at Dagon.

"You bonded her to you, yet your chest is still empty."

Huh?

Dagon throws back his head, shaking out his long hair. "I only just finalized our bond, my lord."

"Ah. In that case, allow me to summon Candor for you. He will mark you as your female's for all of Sombra to see for when you do return to your people."

I'm so confused. Squinting a little, I focus on Duke Haures's chest. Before, I noticed it was kind of shimmering, almost like he had some tinsel standing out against his pale skin. Looking closer, I see that there are... letters?

S-U-S-A-N-N-A.

Oh. He, uh... that must be the traditional tattoos that the demons get. Not a silly little rose like I have on my hip, but the names of their mates.

And he thinks that Dagon wants to carve up his chest the same way so that it says **SIERRA** on it—

"I do," murmurs my mate, glancing down at me. "I am proud to be your male. Not only that, but a hunter is territorial. I want all to know that I am yours—and that you are mine." He lifts his arm, allowing my hand to fall back to my side as he rubs his thumb along the edge of my jaw. "But that can wait. First, your kin."

I nod, and Dagon turns back toward the duke and Susanna. "We are here because my mate is searching for her kin. We think that she might be in Sombra."

Susanna gasps softly. Duke Haures uses his free hand to pat hers, his palm so big, it covers both of them.

"So it's true," she says, more to her mate than to me and mine. "I always thought... it does run in families, doesn't it? The magic—and being destined to be a Sombra demon's mate."

"My mate's kin is bonded to another hunter," explains Duke Haures. "Amelia was meant for Nox just like Su was born in another realm to be mine."

That's nice, and I'd be a lot more interested in that if I knew what the hell happened to Billie.

"Her name is Billie. She's not my blood relative or anything, but she's still my family. And we're not sure she's here, but Dagon said that a guard called Glaine came to my apartment and—"

"I am aware."

Hang on—

"That Glaine broke into my place?"

The duke's eyes glow brighter at my accusatory tone. "Yes. And that he took the mortal, Billie, back to Sombra with him."

He did? "Great. Where is she?"

Duke Haures glances over at Susanna. "I had her put in the dungeons."

Next to me, Dagon tenses up. A flash of a memory skitters across my brain, of seeing Susanna curled up on a stone floor, tucked behind a set of bars, while my claws—*Dagon*'s claws—curl around them, vowing he'll see her out of there.

Because Duke Haures tossed his own mate in the dungeons...

I shake my head. If I let myself, I'll dig deeper, trying to learn a suddenly very intriguing backstory of Susanna and Haures. I don't have time for that. If Billie's in those very same dungeons now...

My hands go to my hips. "What? Is that what you do to human women here? Toss 'em in demon prison?"

Duke Haures purses his lips, making his tusks even more noticeable than before. "She broke my first law. Humans aren't allowed to know about Sombra."

Me and Susanna are proof that there are exceptions. "Yeah. But mates can."

And please, please, please let it be that Billie is a Sombra demon's mate.

That's the one outcome I'd held out hope for more than the rest ever since Dagon suggested that—in what would be the world's biggest coincidence—maybe Billie is Glaine's one true mate. That the guard didn't need to be summoned to her side, that when she came home and he somehow appeared in the apartment at the same time... he just knew she was meant to be his.

Considering Sombra demons are loyal to their mates and so determined to find the one woman meant for them that they'll wait *centuries* for their true love, that option was way better than any other reason the guard might've had to snatch her.

And I get to cling to that hope for maybe two seconds more before Duke Haures blows a breath out through his nose.

"The mortal female was very insistent that she is not a mate."

Yup. That sounds like Billie all right.

"But, my lord," cuts in Dagon, "you are a bondmaster—"

"And she is a human who was brought to our

realm against her will because one of my soldiers wanted his one true mate, but didn't trust in the magic or his future bond enough to wait. And now she denies him."

Dagon frowns. "So Sierra's kin *is* Glaine's mate?"

Good question.

Bondmaster... what the hell is a bondmaster? I ask the question inside my mind, and Dagon's essence answers it because, suddenly, I know that Duke Haures is so different from the rest of the demons in his realm because of his ability to sense—and to sever—fated mate bonds.

Glaine took Billie. Is that why?

"Only the matefinder spell can answer that question for sure."

"Verus amor," murmurs Susanna.

The spell.

The *book*.

"Are you talking about the *Grimoire du Sombra*?"

When neither Duke Haures nor Susanna look surprised that I mentioned it, I admit, "I still have it."

And, hey, if it turns out that Billie is supposed to have a Sombra demon of her own—a guy like Dagon, but one who's perfect for her—there's no way I can just hop a portal back to New York without trying to help her first.

"It's back at my place in the city," I tell them. "I can grab it, bring it back through the portal. She can read it... she'll be a mate... and there's no reason for her to be in the dungeon."

After that, it's up to Billie what she wants to do. But, first, I'm breaking her out, one way or another.

Until the damn demon duke dashes my hopes *again*.

"You could do that, but it would be a waste of a portal. The mortal is gone." Duke Haures waits a beat, then adds, "And so is my top guard."

"What? Where are they?"

"I have my best mages searching since they escaped, but Glaine has been able to evade them so far."

Okay. *Okay.*

I want to make sure I understand because something... this doesn't seem right. Forget the all-powerful duke losing his prisoners. I'm a little stuck on how Billie could get grabbed by the guard, taken to Sombra, thrown into the demon duke's dungeons, and already have escaped long enough for the duke to be sending his wizards to search for them? I mean, it's been... what? Four, maybe five hours since I noticed she was gone.

My confusion must travel right down my bond to Dagon because he does his best to explain it to me.

"Time works differently between realms," he says. "The gold moon is the only way to tell it's passing."

I wish that helped more than I did.

Wow. I must look really lost because it's Duke Haures's turn to take pity on me.

He steeples his claws, looking over the top of those monsters as he says, "It's been four moons since the other mortal crossed into our realm."

Four *moons*? Like, four months?

What?

The human woman clears her throat. "Four nights, my love."

Okay. That's better than thinking Billie's been missing in this demon world for four months, but still. Four nights? If a couple of hours in New York meant four days in Sombra, how much time is passing now? Minutes—or longer? You'd think that, considering I've traveled all over the world thanks to my career, I'd understand the concept. Nope. Time zones make my head spin, and that's on Earth.

My plan was to follow Dagon to his world, expect the all-powerful ruler to retrieve Billie for me, then bring her home. In and out and back home for dinner.

Now? I'm not so sure about that.

Dagon's thinking along the same lines as I am. And it only adds to my growing affection for my demon that his first thought is for Three.

"Your creature, my mate," he murmurs. "Three. We must return to him."

He's not wrong. I have to make arrangements for my—*our*—cat. But after that...

"You're right. Then we're coming back again to help look."

"Sierra?"

It's in the way he rumbles my name, and how he cocks his head slightly, watching me with his unblinking gaze.

Yeah, yeah. I know. I made a big deal about not being ready to give up the glitz and the glamour, the fans and the fame, and while he could tap right into my essence and tell that I'm full of shit—saying what I thought someone like me should instead of being honest about how I really felt—the truth is that I have a job to do. I'm going to do it, but not before I do everything I can to rescue Billie first.

And if that means taking a trip to Sombra to track her down, then that's what I'll do.

I owe her that much. For all the years she stood by me, it's my turn to be there for Billie.

Luckily for me, I have the best bodyguard to help me search the demon world to find my best friend.

"I've got a month before I'm back to work, prepping for my tour to start up again. That should be enough time for me to find Billie and bring her home again."

Dagon takes my hand in his, careful to curve his pointed claws around my fingers. "For us to find her."

I glance up at him. I had hoped he'd be willing to help me, and I'm grateful for his reaction. Still, he's so solemn—and, damn it, Sierra Landry is still way too insecure—that I can't help but ask, "Because you're my shadow?"

Am I teasing a little, trying to hide my growing worry for Billie? Maybe.

And maybe I need to know that, when Dagon says 'forever', he really means it.

A pulse of pure love fills me up at the same time as he rumbles out, "Because I am your mate, Sierra."

Oh.

I breathe out softly.

He's not done.

Dagon gives my hand a gentle squeeze. "Wherever you go, I will be there. Not because I'm indebted to you, or because the gods told me I must. I will be there for all eternity because I love you, and I've waited centuries to take my place behind you."

I didn't think it was possible a few seconds ago, not with everything that has happened today, but my lips quirk into a small, crooked grin that's nothing like the one that's graced a thousand magazine covers.

That's Whiskey Rose.

With Dagon, I can be Sierra—and I fucking love it.

Just like I'm pretty sure I'm halfway to being completely in love with him... or maybe all the way.

"No, demon," I murmur, turning so that my big mate is all I see. So we have a crowd of two watching us... I'm used to being the center of attention, and with Dagon's red gaze blazing down on me, it's easy to forget the duke and his mate are there. "Not behind me. Right beside me."

He lays his other hand on my side, instinctively finding my rose tattoo as he holds me close. "I promise you this: there is nowhere else I'd rather be."

And considering our bond is unbreakable, that's exactly where he'll stay. Whether in Sombra as we search for my best friend, or back in Manhattan, curling up on our bed with Three snuggling at our feet... we'll be together forever.

Heart barely used?

More like heart *stolen*—and claimed by my new mate.

Sierra, I
CLAIMED BY

Sierra
on, & Three
E CREATURE

Help! I've been abducted by a... *demon*?

As if the weekend wasn't enough of a disaster already, right on the heels of discovering how my boyfriend really feels about my best friend, I walk into our apartment—and straight into a trap.

Is it a surprise that I initially think that was meant for her, too? That when I get grabbed and pulled through a portal by a massive demon with *horns*, he mistook me for Sierra?

Only... he didn't. And when he stuns me by

speaking English, he explains that his name is Glaine, and he's my fated mate.

Do I believe him? Of course not. Demon or human, after what happened with Trevor, I was ready to swear men off for good. Besides, he might be sure that I'm his, but how does he know?

And how am I supposed to get back to New York?

I'm determined not to fall for the grumpy demon, especially when my first escape attempt lands me in the dungeons, with Glaine as my cellmate. We're chained together, even after he breaks us out of there, and all I want to do is get away from him... which would be a lot easier if he wasn't dedicated to proving that I'm the mate for him—and he's the guy for me.

Grabbed by the Guard is the sixth book in the **Sombra Demons** series. It tells the story of Billie and Glaine, a stubborn city girl and the demon guard who wanted a mate so badly, he stole her... and is ready to do whatever it takes to keep her.

...

Releasing on August 26, 2024!

Everyone knows that the dark forest of Blackmoor has monsters... but what about demons?

When I'm given the opportunity to petition a "wish" from the Blackmoor council, I'm not so sure I believe in magic—but I'm desperate enough for an escape from my current life to give it a try. Besides, I'm a kick-ass survivalist with a can-do attitude. Despite the rumors and the stories about this "magical" place, there isn't anything in the woods that I can't handle.

Tell that the the toothy little gnomes that attack my first night in...

At least, that's what I call them. Because if I admitted what they really are—freaking Christmas *elves*—I might just think better about spending my holidays in the dark, snowy woods.

With only the clothes on my back and the fruit the Blackmoor council gave me, I decide to find shelter to hunker down and make it through my three days in peace—until those damn elves attack again, intent on bringing me to a ominous man known only as the Toymaster.

But before those creeps can, another demon steps out of the woods, frightening off the elves and scaring the crap out of me.

Krampus is more than six feet tall—not counting his horns—and he looks like he could snap me in half... and that's if he doesn't trap me in the chains he has clutched between his claws.

Of course, after he saves me only to take me for himself, I spend Christmas Eve with Krampus—and those very same chains.

But that's Christmas Eve.

What happens on Christmas? What happens when the Toymaster comes searching for me himself?

And, most importantly, what happens when my three days are done?

Just in time for Christmas in July, you can pre-order your copy of *Christmas Eve with Krampus* now with a release date of July 24th!

KEEP IN TOUCH

Stay tuned for what's coming up next! Follow me at any of these places—or sign up for my newsletter—for news, promotions, upcoming releases, and more!

SarahSpadeBooks.com
Sarah's Newsletter
Sarah's Signed Book Store

facebook.com/sarahspadebooks
x.com/stressie
instagram.com/sarahspadebooks
amazon.com/author/sarahspade

ALSO BY SARAH SPADE

Holiday Hunk

Halloween Boo

This Christmas

Auld Lang Mine

I'm With Cupid

Getting Lucky

When Sparks Fly

Holiday Hunk: the Complete Series

Claws and Fangs

Leave Janelle

Never His Mate

Always Her Mate

Forever Mates

Hint of Her Blood

Taste of His Skin

Stay With Me

Never Say Never: Gem & Ryker

Bound by the Moon

Sombra Demons

Drawn to the Demon Duke*

Mated to the Monster

Stolen by the Shadows

Santa Claws

Bonded to the Beast

Fated to the Phantom

Claimed by the Creature

Grabbed by the Guard

Taken by the Twins

Stolen Mates

The Alpha's Heart*

The Feral's Captive

Chase and the Chains

The Beta's Bride

Wolves of Winter Creek

Prey

Pack

Predator

Protector

Claws Clause

(written as Jessica Lynch)

Mates *free*

Hungry Like a Wolf

Of Mistletoe and Mating

No Way

Season of the Witch

Rogue

Sunglasses at Night

Ain't No Angel

True Angel

Ghost of Jealousy

Night Angel

Broken Wings

Of Santa and Slaying

Lost Angel

Born to Run

Uptown Girl

A Pack of Lies

Here Kitty, Kitty

Ordinance 7304: the Bond Laws (Claws Clause Collection #1)

Living on a Prayer (Claws Clause Collection #2)

Diamonds are a Witch's Best Friend (Claws Clause Collection #3)

www.ingramcontent.com/pod-product-compliance
Lightning Source LLC
Chambersburg PA
CBHW022105310726
48972CB00007B/1897